W9-BYG-122

No Known
Address

No Known Address

Steven Barwin

James Lorimer & Company Ltd., Publishers
Toronto

James Lorimer & Company Ltd., Publishers acknowledges funding support from
the Ontario Arts Council (OAC), an agency of the Government of Ontario. We
acknowledge the support of the Canada Council for the Arts, which last year
invested $153 million to bring the arts to Canadians throughout the country.
This project has been made possible in part by the Government of Canada and
with the support of Ontario Creates.

Cover design: Gwen North
Cover image: Shutterstock

9781459415577
eBook also available 9781459415553
Cataloguing data for the hardcover edition is available from Library and
Archives Canada.

Library and Archives Canada Cataloguing in Publication (Paperback)

Title: No known address / Steven Barwin.
Names: Barwin, Steven, author.
Series: SideStreets. Description: Series statement: Sidestreets
Identifiers: Canadiana (print) 20200246410 | Canadiana (ebook) 20200246429 |
ISBN 9781459415546 (softcover) | ISBN 9781459415553 (EPUB)
Classification: LCC PS8553.A7836 N65 2020 | DDC jC813/.54—dc23

Published by:
James Lorimer &
Company Ltd., Publishers
117 Peter Street, Suite 304
Toronto, ON, Canada
M5V 0M3
www.lorimer.ca

Distributed in Canada by:
Formac Lorimer Books
5502 Atlantic Street
Halifax, NS, Canada
B3H 1G4

Distributed in the US by:
Lerner Publisher Services
1251 Washington Ave. N.
Minneapolis, MN, USA
55401
www.lernerbooks.com

Printed and bound in Canada.
Manufactured by Marquis in Toronto, Ontario in August 2020.
Job #355206

To those who have struggled to find a place they can call home.

Chapter 1

Spinning

I was standing in the kitchen.

My dad looked at me like I was a stranger, a stranger he didn't want to know. It was a look I had become really used to.

Dad stood there in his neatly pressed suit. He swirled a gold-coloured drink around in one of the heavy crystal glasses that he prized. "Give it to me," he finally said.

I squeezed my biology test tightly in my hand.

"Tyler," he said sharply.

I extended the test to him carefully, as if it was a time bomb. Then I waited for the *kaboom*.

He glanced at the mark and grimaced like he had tasted something awful. Then he held it out to me, pointing at the sixty-four written on the top of the page. "What happened to the other thirty-six per cent?"

"I'm sorry." I sighed.

"Are you stupid? Or just plain crazy? Let me see if I can put this in simple terms that even you can understand. You get bad marks, you're worth nothing in this world. And I didn't raise you to be a loser."

I should have been used to it, but his harsh words cut deep.

"It's disgusting," he went on. "This is the kind of mark the junkies who show up at my emergency room got before they dropped out of school. And you have even less excuse than they do. You have had every advantage. So how am I supposed to explain that my son," he spat out the word, "is worse than some strung-out street kid?"

My whole life, I wanted to be just like my dad. I wanted to go to medical school and become an emergency room doctor, just like him. I wanted to help people, to save people the way he did. And for a long time, Dad seemed happy to have me follow in his footsteps. Then things changed. Suddenly, nothing I did was right. No matter how hard I tried, he demanded more. And when I couldn't meet those demands, he punished me and told me what a waste of his time I was.

"Now that I think about it," Dad said shortly, "this could be a very good thing. I owe you a thank you."

I didn't fall for the bait.

"It's clear you won't be needing your college fund, Tyler. That leaves more money for your mother and me."

My mom had always been anxious, but things got much worse in the last couple years.

At first, she stopped shopping and making family dinners. Then she stopped going out at all. When she started staying in bed all day, Dad got worse. I guess helping patients at work and having one at home was too much. Because he was spending more and more time at work, Dad hired a home nurse to look after Mom.

The worse Mom got, the more impossible Dad was to be around. If we were in the same room too long, he'd end up screaming at me. I used to be able to stand it. But after a while I'd come home for food and to see Mom only when Dad was at work. So Dad got the nurse to rat me out every time I came home to see Mom. I'm sure he paid her extra to keep control of his house when he wasn't there.

I turned to walk away. Maybe if I wasn't there to insult, he would forget how much I disappoint him.

"Where do you think you're going?"

I turned, but I couldn't meet his critical stare.

"I've just about given up on you," he said. "And who else would want you? Look at yourself. You can't even clean or dress yourself properly. I'm ashamed to have people know you are even related to me."

Dad loosened his tie and emptied his glass. "I've had a long day at the hospital." He slammed my imperfect test down and went to the liquor cabinet to pour himself another drink. "I guess you know you get no allowance this week. Why should I pay you if I'm not getting anything back? And you're grounded. I want you in your room and that door shut."

Grounded again? I thought. *Who gets grounded at sixteen?* But I knew I was lucky I didn't get below 60 per cent on that test. The last time that happened, I was locked in my room over the whole weekend.

This isn't a home, I thought as I trudged up the stairs. It was just a house with four walls and no heart. And locks that kept me in instead of keeping me safe. What it was, was a prison.

I waited a half hour in my room so Dad could drink enough to not notice I was gone. Then I moved slowly out of my room and down the stairs. I checked that his study light was on before I slipped out the front door.

Chapter 2

Stray Dog

I wanted to storm away from the house in anger. Instead I scurried away. Sometimes I wished, just one time, he'd get angry enough — or drunk enough — to punch me. Then I'd have bruises I couldn't hide. Then people would know the kind of house I lived in.

My cell phone lit up the darkness around me. There was no response from Lucy yet. As I got to her house, I texted her one more time. It wasn't easy coming here to beg, but it was better than home.

Lucy had told me that her parents were okay with me showing up at their home late. But I knew from the way Mrs. Jackson looked at me that Lucy was way off. Mr. Jackson was nicer to me, but only when his wife wasn't around. But I was out of options. I needed a place to crash for the night, so I took a deep breath and knocked on the door.

It opened and right away I sensed that whatever they had for dinner was good. Lucy's mom stood at the door, checking her watch. I didn't know if she'd just stand there until I left or if she'd shut the door in my face. She finally broke the silence by announcing to the house that I was here.

I heard Lucy take the stairs fast. She appeared at the door a little out of breath. Just seeing her, I felt better.

She tucked her straight blonde hair back behind her ears. "Was he drinking?" she whispered, coming out the door a step. Lucy was the only one I'd told about how hard my dad was on me. Even my best friend Simon didn't know.

I nodded.

Lucy gave me a hug.

"I can't talk to him anymore," I told her.

"I'm so sorry you have to deal with all of this."

"He doesn't like me. He'd be a lot happier if I was gone."

"You're a good person, Tyler. You don't owe him anything other than being yourself."

"To him that's not good enough." I couldn't believe I had a girl like Lucy I could turn to. She was more than I deserved.

"Let me ask my mom if you can stay over," she said.

"You sure?"

"Tyler, you've done it before. It's not the biggest deal."

All I needed was their couch to lie down on. I'd even take the floor. Anything to keep from having to sleep on the ground outside or, even worse, going back home. The Jackson home was warm and inviting. Their family room had two big couches facing a TV that was mounted over a real wood-burning fireplace. The mantel was covered with family photos.

I leaned in at the door. I could hear Lucy and her mom arguing about me. Her mom was asking how many times I was going to sleep over.

I blurred out their voices and imagined the family gathering around the kitchen table for dinners and conversation. Everyone probably cared how each other's day was.

"You again."

I snapped to reality as Lucy's brother, Brandon, walked by. He was holding a big bowl of popcorn. He scooped some into his mouth and managed to smirk at me around his chewing.

"What does my sister see in you?" He grabbed more popcorn and held it in front of his mouth. "That's right. She could never say no to a stray dog." He laughed.

I stood there. What could I say? Maybe he was right. I used to be a fun, let's-go-to-a-movie boyfriend. But now all I did was hang around and wait for Lucy to take pity on me. Yep, that's exactly what I was. A stray dog.

Brandon stared at me, my discomfort growing. Then he waved his hand in front of his face. "Shower much? You smell like a dog too!" He barked loudly at me. Then he walked away, still laughing.

Lucy returned to me with a soft smile. She said I could sleep on the couch.

I entered the house, took off my shoes, and walked to the family room. Lucy's mom kept an eye on me as Lucy gave me a sheet and pillow. I whispered to Lucy, "He's getting worse. Angrier at me."

She knew I was talking about my dad. "What are you going to do, Tyler?"

"I don't know. He grounded me. As far as he knows, I'm in my room."

Mrs. Jackson was slowly cutting the lights.

Lucy hugged me. "Sleep well." She leaned in to give me a kiss, but her mom cleared her throat loudly to remind us she was there. I knew Mrs. Jackson didn't trust me. And I didn't blame her. If my dad didn't trust me, how could she? I was nothing to her but a bad boyfriend to her daughter.

I said goodnight to Lucy, and called out a thank you to her mom even though she was already upstairs. Another night out of my house and away from my bed.

This is okay, I told myself, *safety over comfort*.

Chapter 3

Burned Toast

I sat on the couch as the house got quiet, fast. I thought about getting up and searching for food in the kitchen. But I needed to wait until I knew Mrs. Jackson was asleep. She probably catalogued everything so she'd know what I took.

I stood and looked at the pictures on display next to the TV. I'd seen them the last time I was here, but I still liked to look. The Jackson family posed at the Golden Gate

Bridge on a trip to San Francisco. There was another one of them skiing in Whistler. I especially liked seeing photos of Lucy growing up. I checked over my shoulder — was Mrs. Jackson there? But it was just my imagination.

When I figured enough time had passed, I moved to the kitchen. I had to make sure not to leave any evidence of whatever I took to eat. A banana left a peel, a granola bar left a wrapper. I found some cookies in a cupboard and ate them quickly over the garbage can.

I returned to the couch and checked my phone before turning it off. I put my head down, but couldn't sleep. My mind raced about everything that was going wrong with my life. About my dad. He had always had a serious side to him. We never ran around playing football or anything. And he loved his work, so he worked a lot. I always found it funny that he spent all day helping other people but, when he got home, he was too tired for us.

I lifted the blanket to my shoulders and

tried to calm my mind. But whenever I could get myself to stop thinking about what a problem I was for my dad, his voice would take over. It drowned out my inner voice.

***

I woke to the smell of coffee and the sound of chatter. I lurched up off the couch. The Jackson family — minus Lucy — was starting their day. How did I sleep in?

Brandon was the first to speak. "So, what? He's living here now?"

I stood there, exposed to their prying eyes, then turned back to the couch. Feeling their eyes on my back, I yanked the sheets and pillow off the couch and put the cushions back in place.

Mr. Jackson pointed a knife covered in jam. "Just leave them there," he said. "I'll take care of it. Hungry, Tyler?"

Mrs. Jackson had a coffee canister in one hand and her keys in the other. I really didn't want Lucy's parents to think I was a loser. But I couldn't blame Mrs. Jackson for thinking the worst of me.

Lucy arrived in the kitchen and everyone turned to look at her. "What? What did I miss?" she asked.

"Mom and Dad are thinking of adopting Tyler," Brandon said. "That means your boyfriend would be your brother. And that's just disgusting."

"Shut up, Brandon. I already have a disgusting brother."

Mrs. Jackson glared at them, then announced, "Tyler, Lucy will meet you at school."

"Mom!"

She repeated, this time slowly, "Lucy will meet you at school."

I moved to the door and shoved my feet into my shoes. When my hand was on the front door handle, Mr. Jackson said to me quietly, "I'm not going to pretend to know what you're going through. Just know that everyone is figuring it out as they go and no one really knows what the heck is going on."

I nodded.

Then he handed me a piece of toast in a napkin. He said, "It's a little burned, so I added extra jam." He patted me on the shoulder as I went through the door.

I stepped outside and wondered if Brandon was still making fun of me. I didn't like him from the time I first met him at school. I was surprised and irritated when I learned he was Lucy's brother. But my interest in Lucy was greater than my dislike of him.

When I got to Oak Bay High, I took the side entrance. I walked the long hallway past the music rooms toward my locker.

Simon was waiting for me at my locker. I looked like a slob beside him. His shirt was always tucked in. Same went for his life, which was neatly in order. Everything had a spot, whether binders or friendships. "Hey, Argon."

He called me that because he was a science freak. Simon was proud to have memorized all 118 elements in the periodic table. But I was not in the mood for his quirky humour. The only thing on my mind was food and more sleep.

"Remind me, Simon. I'm Argon because?"

"You're gassy."

"And you know what you are?" I asked. "Moron."

Simon paused. "I think you mean Boron."

I smiled. "Sure."

"So I know things between you and your dad have been rocky lately —"

I cut him off before he could ask exactly how rocky. "We're just going through a phase."

"You guys should go to a movie. You used to do that all the time."

I nodded instead of answering.

"Anyway, and I know that school is the last thing on your mind . . ." He held up a neatly stapled stack of paper. "English essay. Big term-one mark. Did you remember it?"

I buried my head in my hands. "I didn't forget. I didn't even know about it."

"But I reminded you, Tyler. I texted you about it. Your dad is going to freak out. Medical school. Remember?"

"Yeah, yeah. You should go to medical school, Simon. You become an ER doctor like my dad."

"I couldn't handle all the blood. Why don't you have your dad talk to the teacher or write a medical note?"

"Nah."

"Then ask for an extension."

"More like beg for one," I said. "Are you free after school, Simon?"

"Need a place to hang out?"

"No. I need to go somewhere and I don't want to go alone."

"Okay."

The bell rang and I followed Simon to class. Then I made a sharp turn into the boys' restroom. I leaned against the sink and looked at my reflection in the mirror. I saw the stray dog looking back at me.

Chapter 4

Rudderless

The bus wheels squealed as we came to a stop near downtown Victoria. Simon and I stepped out into the spitting rain.

"You can tell me where we're going," he said.

I ignored him and tried to stay focused on tracking the address. Too little sleep and too little food made it hard for me to concentrate. We walked along Yates Street, which was lined with antique-looking street lamps. I led him past coffee shops, expensive restaurants, and clothing shops. *It can't be here*, I thought. *Not in the middle of this nice neighbourhood.*

I waited for a break in traffic and crossed the street toward a two-storey, red brick building. On the main floor was a patio restaurant serving Caribbean food. To the right was the alley I was looking for. Each step we took down the narrow laneway took us further into the unknown.

Why did I come here? There is no easy way out of this. Just turn around and go home, I told myself. Around me, windows were protected by iron bars. The alley finally came to an intersection. On the corner was an entrance blocked by a security gate.

"Tyler?" Simon sounded nervous.

I nodded. "This is it." The walls were painted with bright-coloured polka dots scattered around a large rainbow.

Simon stepped closer to me. "This is what?"

I pointed. "The Victoria Youth Centre."

"You serious?" Simon asked.

"This isn't easy for me," I told him. "I'm burning through places to couch hop. I can't stay with you anymore. I've got maybe one or two more nights at Lucy's. I've become very good at figuring out when I'm no longer wanted."

"But I spoke to my parents —"

"Simon, I'm not blaming you. I get it." I reached and pushed a call button by the gate. After a moment I heard a buzz and noticed the door camouflaged in the rainbow paint. "You can go home if you want. I understand," I said before going in.

Inside, a large sign instructed me to take off my shoes. I stepped onto a carpet and down a short hallway. Simon followed me into a room filled with a bunch of mismatched couches facing an old TV.

"Hello, there." I turned to see a woman. Her dark brown hair was hanging in two braids and she wore fur-lined moccasins with a coloured beadwork design.

"My name is Wenonah," she said. "I'm a counselor here. What is your name?"

"Tyler," I answered. "And this is my friend Simon."

"How can I help you, boys?"

I didn't know what to say, even though my mind was full of questions. *Can I just ask for a place to stay when I need it? Do you have to speak to my dad first?*

"Let me start by saying this shelter is a safe and caring space for anyone thirteen to nineteen years old. It's also a drop-in and hangout space whenever you need." She started to give us the tour.

I saw people my age fast asleep on benches. As we stepped farther in, I noticed more kids asleep or zoned out on the mismatched couches. Some had tattoos running up their necks or on their hands. One girl was muttering to herself angrily. *How is this a safe place?* I wondered.

"There's an evening meal program," Wenonah was saying. "And shower and laundry facilities. We also have drop-in counselling. Would this be for you?"

Simon waved her off and pointed to me. "For Tyler," he said.

"Yeah, maybe . . ." I said.

Wenonah smiled. She paused for me to finish. Since she seemed like she'd be a good listener, I continued, "Do you call parents?"

"Are you over fifteen?"

"I'm sixteen."

"In your case, no. Everyone you see here left home for different reasons. Some have families facing financial hardships. Others are recovering from physical and emotional abuse, and some have parents who are drug abusers. And if it's not that, it's often a parent who doesn't accept their child's sexual orientation. You know, lesbian, gay, bisexual, transgender, queer, or two spirited."

"So," Simon asked, "these people live here? Permanently?"

"Unfortunately, no," replied Wenonah. "This is short-term, emergency housing. Just to help people over a rough patch."

Rough patch, I thought. *Is that what I'm going through?*

We continued to walk around.

"There are some questions I need to ask you, Tyler. It's part of intake."

"Okay."

"Have you been living on the street?"

"I've been bouncing around?"

"Have you done any sex work?"

"What? No!" *Is that what people here have done?* I wondered.

"What about drugs?"

"No."

She showed us a room with some bunk beds. "Everyone here goes through a medical screening."

I was glad she didn't know where I came from. A large house with a three-car garage and beachfront. When the weather was clear I could see Port Angeles and Mount Olympus peeking above Washington State from across the strait.

I looked around the small place with faded furniture.

"I'd be happy to set up a time to talk," prompted Wenonah. "We can start now if you'd like?"

The last thing I wanted was to talk about my problems. Maybe home wasn't so bad. If she was asking about sex work and taking drugs, then I really didn't belong here. It was so far from school I'd be spending most of my time travelling back and forth.

"I can't. Actually, I think I'm okay."

Wenonah looked at me with concern. "Maybe later? I'm always available." She handed me a brochure. "You're welcome back any time, Tyler."

I hurried Simon out of there. He didn't seem to want to stay any longer than I did.

Back in the alley I took in a deep breath of fresh air. I asked Simon, "So, what do you think?"

Simon smiled nervously. "I can't believe that my best friend whose dad is a doctor has to even look at a place like this."

"Imagine how I feel!"

"You said things weren't that bad."

"You're right, Simon. They aren't this bad. I guess I just wanted to look."

"Okay," Simon said. After a short silence he said, "You should've asked if they had Wi-Fi."

I looked at him. Was he for real?

"Yeah, you're right."

After all, I hadn't told Simon the way things were at home. It wasn't his fault that he didn't know I had nowhere to turn.

Chapter 5

Not Welcome

I arrived at Lucy's house greeted by a blank look from Mrs. Jackson. *Where is the sneer at my unchanged clothes? My greasy hair?* I wondered.

She said, "I'll give you one thing. Your arrival time is consistent."

Was that an underhanded compliment? My timing was exact because I didn't want to interrupt the Jacksons' family time.

"Come on in."

Did she actually invite me in? I followed her

cautiously to the dining room. Lucy was doing homework. She looked up at me and closed her textbook with a thud. Her eyes looked empty, like after her grandfather died.

Mr. Jackson arrived with a hot cup of tea for me. He gave me the smallest of smiles and sat down.

I sank into my seat. This looked like some sort of intervention. But I fell for it, hanging there like a stupid fish on a hook just reeled onto the boat.

"So," Mr. Jackson started, "there are some things we'd like to discuss."

Mrs. Jackson leaned forward, her sharp elbows seeming to dig into the wooden table. "We spoke to your father. Dr. Frye."

My face met my hands halfway and buried itself in them.

Mrs. Jackson asked, "Tyler, can you hear me?"

Lucy said, "He can hear you, Mom."

I ran my hands up my face and through

my hair. I had only one thought. *Run.* I got up, but that seemed to anger the Jacksons. I sat back down.

What's next? I wondered. *Is Brandon going to storm in and hold me down?*

Mrs. Jackson tried again. "He sat where you're sitting and —"

My voice grew loud. "My dad was here?"

"We wanted to have Dr. Frye over to talk. He should know where you've been hiding at night."

I groaned. It made me sick to my stomach that they went to him behind my back.

Mr. Jackson was clearly the good cop in their good cop/bad cop routine. "Tyler, your dad cares about you. He's genuinely worried."

"You had no right," I protested. "This is my life. You shouldn't have called him. You can't trust what he has to say."

Mrs. Jackson nodded. "He said you might say something like that."

I jumped up, pushing my chair behind me.

"Now, hold on," Mr. Jackson said. He held both hands level with the table. "I get what you're saying, Tyler." He pushed on despite the glares from Mrs. Jackson. "You're going through a difficult time. We're not judging you." He smiled. "Sit down."

I continued to stand there. Growing confusion mixed with anger. *Am I that bad a person? Do I have a face that screams, "Don't trust this guy"?*

Believe it or not, I had liked spending time at the Jacksons'. Once I got past the front door grilling, they left me alone and didn't pry . . . until now.

Mrs. Jackson pointed at me and then tapped her finger on the table. "You made it about us when you slept on our couch. Over and over again."

I looked to Lucy for a lifeline. Her arms were folded and her hoodie was covering some of her face. She must have been ordered by her mother to keep her mouth shut.

"Tyler," Mrs. Jackson continued, "Dr. Frye has a very different story from the one you've been feeding Lucy."

Lucy jumped in, "It's not like that."

"It is exactly like that, Lucy," her mom retorted. "You said sleeping at home was not an option for Tyler. But that's a lie. Isn't it?" Mrs. Jackson had me in her crosshairs. "Tyler, your father is really concerned that you are going to blow up and do something you're going to regret."

I looked at Mrs. Jackson, really looked at her. Suddenly I realized that she might be enjoying my trial. Did she do this to her own kids too?

"Dr. Frye said that you're very rebellious. You're not focused on academics. You're very temperamental. And you are defiant to anything he says." She used her fingers to count off every point.

Stop calling him Dr. Frye, I screamed inside my head. She made it seem like he was a hero, a larger-than-life character. His name was Jack. He was my dad.

Mr. Jackson tried to jump in. "Honey, stop."

"No. He needs to know we know the truth. Is this the kind of person we want in our house? Dating our daughter?"

Mr. Jackson sat back in his chair. He put both hands behind his head.

I had been firmly put in my place. Thanks to my dad, the Jacksons now saw me the same way he saw me. Like a dog. Worse than a dog, because a dog is obedient to its master. *Good going, Tyler*, I thought. I was on a roll. I had burned through two families. "Is that it?" I asked.

"No," Mrs. Jackson shook her head. "Brandon said his headphones went missing the last time you slept here."

"What? Now I'm a thief too?"

Lucy jumped up and angrily pushed her chair in. "I'm not being part of this attack," she said.

While Mrs. Jackson ignored Lucy, Mr. Jackson said, "We're not attacking you, Tyler. We just want to be clear about what's going on."

"Is it true?" Mrs. Jackson demanded.

How could I respond to that? Before I could utter a big, fat no, Brandon burst into the dining room.

"Those red Beats are the best noise-cancelling headphones you can buy!"

He'd been listening in the whole time! The room exploded. A screaming match between brother and sister burst out.

Mr. Jackson stood and restored order.

In the ensuing silence, Mrs. Jackson handed out her final orders to me. "Your couch-hopping days at our house are over."

Brandon smiled at me.

Mr. Jackson attempted to soften the blow. "Whatever's going on, you being here isn't part of a solution. You need to take care of yourself and your dad. Especially with what's going on with your mother. We had no idea."

He told them about my mom? I didn't expect him to play that sympathy card.

Mrs. Jackson nodded. "Just be glad we're not pressing theft charges." She didn't care about my mom at all. "You're not to return to our house again."

As I stepped outside, I could hear Lucy racing upstairs. Then the door closed behind me.

I walked away, furious about the lies my dad fed the Jacksons. And I kept walking, making sure to not look back.

Chapter 6

Spineless

It had happened. The moment I was dreading. I was out on my own. Was this what hitting rock bottom felt like? I knew that I had been wearing thin on the Jacksons. But if it wasn't for my dad, I'd be inside right now. Instead, I was forced to face the cool winds coming off the tides.

Dad had spoken freely about what a bad person I was. Why would my own father not only continually tell me that, but share it with others? Was he right? Maybe if I could talk to him outside of the house, he could hear what I was thinking. Maybe it was time for him to hear how I felt about what was going on. I went home, determined to say something to him, but his car wasn't there.

I turned around. There was only one other place he could be. I made it to the bus just in time and found a seat. It was a slow ride, but I didn't care. It gave me time to plan what I was going to say. Dad was always letting me have it. Now it was my turn.

After making a bus switch, I got close enough to the hospital to walk. A light drizzle and fog blurred my vision. Even as a kid, I could remember visiting Dad and hating hospitals. It was the smell — a mix of floor cleaner and bad food. When the emergency room doors parted, I entered the large waiting area. It was very busy.

Was this a mistake? I wondered. What would I actually say to him if he listened to me? I could ask him why he'd lied to the Jacksons about me. The Jacksons had let me stay and maybe they deserved the truth. My truth. Maybe I should have explained to them what was really going on at home. I continued past a wall of windows labelled *Triage*. Dad once told me that triage is a process to decide which patients got seen first based on how bad they were hurt. I was hurting inside. Where would triage place me?

I followed a paramedic as they pushed a stretcher through double doors. My pace slowed. I was getting nervous. If I didn't find Dad now and try to say what I wanted to say, I'd back down. I'd leave without confronting him. I pushed myself through the busy hallway. I was driven by a toxic fear that everything I was thinking about our situation was wrong. That he was right. That he knew better.

What am I doing here? I questioned. *Can I tell him that I love him? That I don't want to hurt him or Mom anymore?* I was mumbling to myself like a weirdo.

The ER branched out into four wards. I turned left and approached the nurses' station. My breath hitched when I spotted *Dr. Frye* written on a whiteboard. It meant he was working tonight.

Then I spotted his profile at the end of the hallway. He was in his white doctor's coat and holding a clipboard. He was talking to another doctor. My muscles tensed as I imagined him sitting in the Jacksons' home spreading lies about me. I wasn't the kind of son he wanted, but why did he need everyone else to hate me too?

As I watched him, I tried to come up with what I wanted to say. How would I start?

You're probably surprised to see me here. I know I am. I wanted to turn around so many times. Don't be upset that I just showed up at your work.

Get to your point, I told myself. *He's a busy man.*

Okay, here's what I'm trying to say. Dad, everything I do upsets you. I'm not trying to do it.

I want to make you happy, make you proud. But I feel so judged by you. I can't lie — all the things between us add up to a lot of hurt for me. And I know I hurt you and Mom. But I don't see anything I can do that will make it better.

"Tyler?"

A distant voice caught my attention. It took me a moment to snap back to reality, where I was standing in the hospital corridor. Standing still as a statue. The hospital smell flooded back to my senses.

"Tyler."

I turned to see a nurse in a sky-blue uniform standing next to me. "Nurse Taylor."

"You remember me! Everything okay?"

I wiped sweat from my forehead. "Uh, yeah." Half of my brain was still lost in thought.

"Visiting your dad, are you?"

"No." *Chicken!* I couldn't believe that I was chickening out!

She was confused by my answer. "Oh?"

She pointed. "Well, he's right over there. Should I grab him?"

I nodded and Nurse Taylor led me in his direction. She asked me how school was. She blabbed on about how great my dad was. But my brain was still full of the script in my head.

As we got closer to him, chills started streaming through my body, chasing my confidence away.

I didn't realize I had stopped until Nurse Taylor said, "Everything okay, Tyler? You seem out of sorts. Dazed."

Don't be a chicken! I stepped toward Nurse Taylor. "I'm okay."

As she led me toward him, I could see my dad start to turn. And suddenly I knew I couldn't face him. My instinct to run overtook my desire to fight. I darted backward and around a corner.

***

I was long gone from the hospital, but I was still boiling over in frustration. Dad was right about me. All that disappointment he had for me? I was feeling it in myself. I was disgusted with how I had just confirmed everything he had told me over the years. I was spineless. I was useless. I wanted to scream or cry, but I felt like I was nothing more than an empty shell of the Tyler I thought I knew.

Once my panic started to drop down from the red zone, I realized something. I had nowhere to sleep tonight. I thought about riding the bus on its loop all night. But Victoria was a small town and buses stopped running at ten.

I found myself on the steps of Simon's apartment building. I didn't know if he'd let me in. I knew his family didn't have the space for me or the money to feed me. And Simon once told me that his parents didn't have much sympathy for someone like me who came from a nice, big house and never wanted for anything. But I had no one else to turn to and nothing to lose. I was on the street now.

I texted Simon that I was in front of his building. It took a couple of long minutes before he came out of the elevator. He opened the lobby door and the one to the outside.

Before he could say anything, I told him, "It's this or I have to go downtown and see if that shelter has space, which they probably don't."

Simon looked comfortable in track pants and a hoodie. Like he was doing homework or getting ready for bed. "Can you call them?"

"What? Seriously, Simon!"

"Okay, okay." He adjusted his glasses. "What do you want me to do? You know there's no space here."

I turned in my spot and started to walk away. I had reached the sidewalk before Simon said, "Tyler."

I paused, but didn't turn to him.

"My parents just don't understand how you

choose not to live in your giant house with your rich parents." He paused. "I can't bring you upstairs to our apartment. There's no way they won't find or hear you." He held the door open. "But I have an idea."

We rode one floor down in the elevator. He placed his index finger against his lips as we walked to the end of the hallway. He held open a door. "Best I can offer you is here."

I stepped inside. "The laundry room?"

"If the manager finds you and learns how you got in, we can get evicted."

I offered a tired smile. "The laundry room is perfect. I'll get out by the time anyone is up."

"Just be quiet."

"Got it, Simon. Just one more thing."

"What?"

I held up my phone. "Got a charger?"

"I'm not going back upstairs for you." And he left.

I moved through the laundry room. It had a low ceiling and ugly green flooring. Two rows of stacked white machines took up most of the space. I opened and closed each washer and dryer, looking for clothes. I found a towel in one of them. I rolled it into a makeshift pillow and found a spot on the dirty green tile to lie down. After an hour of tossing and turning, I realized that I was hungry.

Alone in the basement of Simon's apartment building, I felt like a ghost.

I sat against a dryer and wedged the towel behind my neck. With tired eyes, I stared at my distorted reflection in the white side of the washer. *Dad just shut me down*, I thought, *without even trying*. I had never felt so unwanted and unloved.

Chapter 7

Clash

School was once my top priority. My focus was on getting good grades and dreaming about med school. Then it became my escape plan. To go to a university far away, like McGill in Montreal or Dalhousie in Halifax. At least that way I'd be disappointing my dad in a different time zone. He'd be happy to have me out of his life and I'd be thrilled to have a home of my own in a residence.

But now university was out of reach. *Forget that plan*, I thought, *you're stuck in day-to-day survival mode*. My top priority was to find a place to sleep and to scavenge for something to eat.

"Didn't hear you leave this morning."

I spoke quietly, grumbling to Simon, "I'm here aren't I?"

"My parents never suspected anything."

"Yep. That's me. Invisible."

"That's the last time."

I nodded. "Got it."

"For real."

"Got it," I repeated.

"What's wrong with you?"

I pressed my thumbs against my eyes and rubbed them. *He wants me to open up? Alrighty then.*

"Simon, I'm in a hole. I've got nothing. People see me and think, why doesn't he just go home? I know you do too." I held up my hand so he couldn't interrupt. "I can't. My dad's a dictator. He locks me in my room for failing tests. He screams at me. He makes me feel like trash every day. He drinks and it gets worse. I see everyone else running around living their lives, thinking my dad is such a great man. I wish, just one time, people could see the good doctor through my eyes. Then they'd know what a drag it is to be me. And that being at home isn't an option."

"I'm sorry." He closed his locker. "Algebra period one. What a great way to start the day."

My best friend was resorting to small talk. Had I become that hard to be around?

My gaze turned to a pack of boys trooping down the hallway. At the front stood the last one I wanted to see, the one responsible for me being evicted from the Jacksons' house.

I left Simon and headed for Brandon. I cut in front of him, forcing him to halt.

He stopped, alarm flashing across his face.

"What's that?" I pointed to the red Beats headphones he had. The ones he had accused me of stealing.

"Oh, these guys. Yeah, I found them. I guess you got nervous and decided to return them." His buddies around him laughed.

"Your parents think I'm a thief."

"And they'll keep thinking that because they'll never see these. They've already ordered me a blue pair." He turned to his friends. "This is the loser I was telling you about. The one who was slumming it up my house."

One of his friends said, "This is the hobo!" They all laughed.

I screamed, "You liar!" I reached for the Beats around Brandon's neck. I got hold of one end and pulled hard.

Startled, Brandon stepped back and tried to swipe my hand away.

I wasn't going to let go. I'd rather break his precious Beats than let them go.

The struggle came to a quick stop when a voice rang out from behind. "Stop it!"

I didn't need to turn to know it was Lucy. I stepped away and enjoyed watching a frazzled

Brandon check to see if his headphones were broken.

"You're crazy, man." As he adjusted them around his neck, I could tell that the ear cover on the side I grabbed had detached.

"You guys really fighting?" Lucy asked.

"He came at me!" Brandon cried shrilly.

"Whatever, Brandon!"

Brandon grinned at me. "Did she tell you the big news?"

"Shut up, Brandon."

He brushed away an invisible tear and offered an insincere, "Nice knowing you, Tyler." Then he gathered his friends to walk away.

Lucy and I were alone in the hallway. "What's your brother talking about?" I asked.

"He's being a jerk. Tyler, my parents don't think it's a good idea, you being around —"

"I know I'm banned from being in your house —"

"That's not what I meant. You've got a lot going on."

"What's going on is completely out of my control." I reached for her. "You of all people know that. And now I need you more than ever."

"That's a lot of pressure to put on me." She moved out of the way of some students heading to class. "It's my mom. She tries to control my life and ends up making things more complicated for me."

"Lucy, you're not breaking up with me, are you?"

She shook her head and wiped away a tear. "You know it's what my mom wants."

I stepped closer to her and held her hand. "What do you want?"

"I want you."

I smiled and hugged her. A wave of relief spread through my body. "And I want you too."

Chapter 8

The Con

I sat in Science class and tried to get my
bearings. My head spun at the thought of
Lucy's mom trying to cut me out of her life.
Why was I constantly being punished for things
that were out of my control?

A thought crept into my brain. *What if
it wasn't her mother?* What if Lucy wanted to
break it off with me and my broken life? Lucy
needed to focus on school and her future, not
my problems.

"Are you going to sample that?"

I turned to see two eyes wrapped in plastic safety goggles looking down at me.

"Huh?"

My lab partner Jeffrey appeared older than everyone in the classroom because of sheer size. He pointed to a large plastic container filled with water we had collected from a marsh behind the school.

I nodded. "Yeah, ready to go."

He held up a small green strainer. "You'll need to use the net to skim up a sample from our aquatic ecosystem."

I put on my safety goggles. "I got this," I said, and submerged my skimmer. It disappeared as I slowly stirred the sample of murky liquid.

Jeffrey rubbed his hands together. "There's got to be an organism or two in there."

After a moment, I lifted the skimmer. It contained a collection of items.

Jeffrey was a dependable lab partner, the

kind of guy who got along with everyone. I could remember a time when I pulled my share of the workload, when I got an A-plus on every project. But that was a long time ago. I felt bad that on this assignment, I couldn't give it my all.

Jeffrey carefully jotted down his observations and the slothful student I had become copied his work, word for word.

I watched him classify our sampling and realized something more crucial than Science class and getting good grades. First I had to prove myself to Jeffrey. I reached deep down for the student I used to be when I got sleep and had square meals. I suggested, "Why don't I create a binomial nomenclature chart so we can have everything we find properly named."

Jeffrey adjusted his goggles and nodded approvingly.

Then I made my move. "Our report for this is due in a couple of days. What do you think about finishing it up after school? That way it's done and out of the way."

I waited. He was busy working and I didn't want to push him. One thing I knew from dealing with the Jacksons — the hard sell never worked.

Jeffrey eventually said, "Good idea."

Then I moved to the next step in my set-up. "We can work at my house." I couldn't seem desperate, even though that's exactly what I was. It was this or sleeping on the street. I looked around the classroom. Did anyone know what I was going through?

"Oh, wait, my mom is having her book club friends over. And they can get pretty loud."

He looked at me.

I continued my notes and then let my words hang. "We can do it another time, unless . . ."

If it didn't work, I could always push a little harder. Then it would seem like all of this was his idea. I was becoming a master manipulator. When I got my target, there was no letting go.

Jeffrey said, "My house is good then."

I contained my relief. "Cool," was all I said.

***

Getting past the front door was my first win. As we went in the kitchen, I saw that the best part of Jeffrey's house was his mom.

"Welcome, Tyler," she said, smiling. "Great to see the two of you are going to tackle that science project."

She even had some healthy snacks out. I looked but didn't touch, waiting for Jeffrey to go first. But he was in no rush because he got the snacks every day.

I stared at a banana and remembered it was like that at the Jacksons' at the beginning. But once I started to settle in, I was the banana, rotting from sitting out too long. Soon fruit flies started buzzing around, and my overstay caused problems.

For now, Jeffrey's home was a fresh start. All they knew was that I was a seemingly normal guy.

We set up at the kitchen table. The moment Jeffrey reached for a handful of grapes, I dove into the snacks head first.

His computer was open. "Can I?" I asked and started to type up the notes from class. My fingers clicked on his computer keyboard, but I was having a hard time focusing. A pot on the stove was bubbling and calling my name. It emitted the smell of really good chili or meatballs or pasta sauce or something. It was driving me crazy.

When Jeffrey's dad arrived, I was invited to stay for dinner. I was happy not to be the one to suggest it. The meatballs were, as predicted, stupendous. I was officially jealous of Jeffrey's life.

"So, tell us about yourself, Tyler," his mom said.

I kept it brief. They, of course, knew of my dad so I focused on the crowd-pleasers. "One day I hope to go to the University of British Columbia's med school and become a doctor just like my dad."

To avoid more prying questions, I excused myself to the bathroom. I needed to be alone and to think. How was it that this family was so perfect and mine was, well, the complete opposite?

I looked at myself in the mirror and compared. Jeffrey's mom prepared a delicious dinner. My mom couldn't prepare toast. Jeffrey's father had a glass of water with dinner. My dad always had a cocktail or three. How were these strangers so kind and accepting of me? I stopped having friends over the moment I had to provide a debrief to Dad of what we did, ate, and said.

I took a deep breath and returned to the table. These kind people thought I was just here for dinner. But I'd been slowly leaving clues that might lead them to invite me to stay. I mentioned that home was a fair distance away. I also told them that my dad went to bed early to be ready for the first shift at the ER. Just as I was starving for dinner, I was hurting for a place to sleep without having to directly ask for it. I reached for the potatoes, hating myself. Dad was right. I was a con, a leech, a liar. And I was cheating Jeffrey's family out of the welcome that I should have had at home.

Chapter 9

Everyone Has a Story

Our science project was sprawled across the dining room table. Jeffrey's excitement for science had me focused on school work and it felt great. I felt normal, even for just a moment.

"Your mom is amazing," I told Jeffrey. "That dinner was amazing!"

Jeffrey kept his focus on the assignment. "Thanks."

"No, really. I'm serious. You're lucky to have a mom like that." I thought about opening up to him. But it was too early in our friendship, if we were even going to be close enough.

"Do you think I look like her?" Jeffrey asked.

"Ah, maybe. I didn't really look."

"If you did, you might see that she's not my mom. Well, she's my mom, but not my mom-mom."

"Your mom isn't your mom?"

Jeffrey turned away from the project and shook his head.

"I'm confused. So, then, what about your dad?"

"Dad-dad? Nope."

"But they're so nice. You're so nice!"

"Tyler, I am a foster kid."

"What? Really?"

"Yeah."

"You mean you don't have parents?"

Jeffrey glanced at me. Was I prying too much?

"I'm sorry. I'm just surprised. But I get it. If I told you what was really going on at my house, you wouldn't believe me."

"You want my story?"

"Sure." The least I could do was listen to Jeffrey's troubles.

"Okay. My parents got divorced. My dad took off so mom had to work two jobs and I basically had to take care of myself. She was stressed and didn't have time for me. I kind of think she blamed me a little."

I can relate to that, I thought.

"Our apartment was disgusting. Because I didn't know how to cook, we weren't eating proper meals."

What were the chances that Jeffrey and I had some things in common?

"My teacher started asking questions. When she found out that I was pretty much taking care of myself, she called child services. They showed up at the apartment. That did not go well."

I wondered if my teachers were concerned about me. A good student's marks tanking should show up on their radar.

"All I wanted was to be free so I wasn't a burden on my mother. I could find a way to take care of myself. But I was too young. You have to be at least sixteen. Next thing I know, the courts got involved and I was placed in foster care."

"This family?"

"Nope. I bounced around different homes. Some were wonderful. Some I just didn't fit in. One year I bounced through three foster families."

"That must've been crazy."

"Very stressful. I acted out in school and got into trouble. What I really wanted was not to be a foster kid anymore."

"You mentioned being free from your home, but you weren't sixteen. How could you be free?"

"We should probably get some work done. Right?"

"No, please. Jeffrey, this is important."

"Why is what happened in my life important?"

"Because I haven't been honest with you."

Jeffrey chuckled. "Yeah, you said something about what's really going on at your house. No book club, eh?'

I didn't know where to start.

He said, "It's called getting emancipated."

"What's that?"

"Basically, you legally separate from your parents. You become free of their custody and control."

Yes! That's what I needed! "But you're sixteen. You could do that now, right? But these people are so nice."

"They are incredibly nice. And yes, my foster mom is an excellent cook. My foster dad makes some mean pancakes too." He paused for a beat. "I can't get emancipated as a foster kid. When I turn eighteen, they call it aging out of the system. Then I'll be out on my own."

I tried to take mental notes as Jeffrey dished out the information I hadn't realized I needed.

Jeffrey went on, "You have to remember that being a foster parent doesn't mean being a parent in the way you're thinking. They are people who officially take a child or teen into their family, but only for a certain period of time. They don't become my legal parents, but they do get paid."

"So they could have another person after you?"

"Yep. They had two before me. They still keep in touch with one of them. Her picture is by the fireplace."

I leaned back in my chair and stared up at the ceiling. My mind was officially blown. When I had thought there was no way out, maybe I was wrong.

"Thanks for sharing, Jeffrey. It means more than you know."

"Now I'm interested. What's your story?"

I thought about how clearly Jeffrey was able to tell his story. How he didn't choke up at parts that were genuinely sad. So I tried to give him the summary, to spare him my sob story. "My dad and I don't get along. He's a difficult guy to please and I'm always messing up in his eyes. My mom's home, but stuck to her bed, so we're dealing with that too."

"That's hard," Jeffrey said.

"Yeah. I guess the main problem is that my dad starts off critical and stern. Then he gets a drink or two in him and it turns to anger."

"Tyler, what you're experiencing might be abuse."

"I never thought about it that way. I just saw it as dealing with life."

I had an urge burning inside me to completely open up and tell the truth. Tell Jeffrey that I was trying to use him so that I'd have a place to stay.

"Jeffrey . . ." I started, while really mulling it over in my mind. But then I chickened out.

"Thanks for listening," I said. I was too afraid that I'd lose Jeffrey as a friend. His story was the first thing that made me feel like I wasn't going through this alone.

"One thing I've learned," Jeffrey started, "is that you can't judge anyone. Because everyone's got their story."

As we returned to the science project, my phone rang. It was Lucy.

"Tyler."

I could sense from her voice that something was wrong. Her tone was frantic. "Lucy, what's going on?"

"I'm at home. You have to come now."

"What? I'm banned —"

"Please!"

"Lucy, I can't."

"My brother threw a party and it's way out of control. My parents aren't home. Tyler, I'm scared. I have no one else to turn to."

"Okay, okay. Just stay there. I'm on my way."

"What is it?" Jeffrey asked.

"My girlfriend. She needs me. I'm sorry, but I have to go."

"Okay. No problem. Mind if I continue working on this?"

I patted him on the back. "You're the best."

I was out the door and hit the sidewalk in full sprint. All I could think about was Lucy being scared. She had done so much for me, I couldn't stay away if she needed me there. I caught the bus just as it was about to leave. I sat close to the door, my foot tapping on the floor, as if that would make the bus go faster.

Chapter 10

Strung Out

I ran up to the Jacksons' house out of breath. The front door was locked. I tried knocking, but there was no answer. Loud music thrummed from inside. But Lucy's emergency was greater than my fear of getting caught in this house.

I reached for my phone to call Lucy to let me in when suddenly the door opened.

A guy I didn't know looked at me, weaving a bit. "Pizza guy's here," he announced.

I blew past him, right into a wall of sound blasting from speakers. The family room was over capacity with bodies everywhere, some pouring over into the dining room. Both rooms were a total mess. Empty beer bottles lay sideways on the coffee table and floor. I focused in on a small open bottle with its cap off. Red and white pills spilled onto the table.

People I recognized from school were strung out on the couch.

I pushed through the crowd and found Brandon at the dining room table. He was sitting where I had been when the Jacksons delivered their marching orders to me.

"Hey, man," he said. He tried to identify me through his bloodshot eyes. He smiled for a beat, and then located my contact information in his brain. Brandon stammered as he spoke, "Look who it is, everyone."

I didn't react. I had a major advantage over everyone in the room. I wasn't stoned, drunk, or buzzed.

Brandon stood clumsily and leaned on me. "It's the . . . loser my . . . sister dumped." It was clear that Brandon was working to communicate through a thick haze.

"Where's Lucy?" I asked.

"Have you come to party? Because you're . . . not invited."

A few people around him chuckled.

I pulled back. Brandon lost his balance and fell back on the chair.

"Where's your sister?" I repeated.

He didn't answer. I found the source of the music and unplugged the wireless speakers. The reaction from the crowd was not good.

Behind me a loud crash rang out, followed by a wave of hard laughter. It was probably something valuable.

"Where's your sister?" I asked once more.

Brandon reached for a nearby bottle of pills and tried to fish one out, even though it was clearly empty.

I moved on. There were people in every

room. There were things broken and broken into. The Jacksons were going to be very upset. Even though I was no longer wanted, I racked my brain for what I could do to help out. I thought about calling the police. But then Brandon would get into even more trouble. Instead I shouted, "Hey, everyone. Party's over. Time to get out!"

People who could looked up, but no one showed any sign of listening. I spotted another bottle of pills on the staircase. It read, *Nancy Sheppard. Take 1–2 tablets every 4–6 hours as required for pain.* Below that was the word *Hydrocodone*.

I placed the bottle on a ledge halfway up the stairs. I stepped cautiously on the second floor and called out, "Lucy?" I pushed on toward her bedroom, opened the door, and stepped inside her room.

"Tyler!" Lucy got up from where she had been slumped on the floor. She stepped around her bed and embraced me. "You came!"

"Are you okay?"

"Yes. I'm so glad you're here. Brandon invited some friends over as soon as my parents left for dinner. I told the idiot he was going to get in trouble," she scoffed. "Then people just started showing up and now it's out of control."

"Have you called your parents?"

"No. I should, right? Because somehow I'm going to get blamed for doing nothing."

"Let's go down and kick them all out. Then we can call your parents."

Lucy nodded. "My brother's taking the fall for whatever's going on down there. This isn't my fault."

"I know. They'll understand."

I knew that Brandon was a jerk who would throw Lucy under the bus for this party if he could. I led Lucy out of her bedroom.

"Is anybody in my parents' room?" she asked. "There better not be anyone in there!"

We cautiously opened the double doors.

The lights were dimmed and two people were on top of the bed.

Before I could do anything, Lucy let them have it.

"Get out, get out!" She flicked the lights to full brightness. "This is my parents' bedroom, you assholes!"

I guess she just needed me at her side to find the confidence to let them have it.

A guy and girl reacted to the change in lights and Lucy's screaming. They didn't seem to be embarrassed that we caught them. Actually, they seemed annoyed that we were interrupting their make-out session.

I repeated Lucy's words as loud as I could: "Get out!" They finally got up and left.

"Help me with the bed, Tyler," Lucy said.

I grabbed the other end of the bed sheets and tried to straighten them. It was beyond weird to be in Mr. and Mrs. Jackson's bedroom making their bed.

Once we were back in the hallway, I said to

Lucy, "I should go. Your parents will kill me if your brother says a word about me being here."

"No, Tyler. I'll tell them you came to help me —"

I interrupted, "You mean your ex-boyfriend just showed up. The one who has been banished from your house."

She paused and smiled. "To them, you can still be my friend."

The situation went from bad to horrible as police sirens blared in the distance, but coming closer.

Chapter 11

Accused

The police siren grew to an angry roar. I could see flickering blue and red lights outside by the time I got downstairs.

It was full panic mode as everyone scattered around Brandon to make a run for it.

Why am I not making a run for it? I wondered. I should've been the first out the back door or a window.

I pressed Lucy to open the front door. She needed to be proactive and show the police that we were on their side.

A police officer took in the situation before saying, "Is there an adult home?" Her uniform and fully packed gun belt were intimidating.

Lucy shook her head no.

"Multiple neighbours put in a complaint about the noise coming from this house."

I raised my hand like I was in school and quickly dropped it. "I turned the music off when I got here."

"And you are?"

"I'm her boyfriend — I mean a friend. This is her house."

Lucy seemed shell-shocked in the presence of the police. "Yes, this is my house."

I kept repeating in my head, *Tyler, why didn't you leave!*

Bright headlights lit up the darkness behind the police officer. My heart dropped and a lump formed in my throat. Too late. It was the Jacksons.

Lucy was relieved to see them. "Mom,

Dad, I'm so glad you're here," she cried.

Mrs. Jackson embraced Lucy, checking her as if to look for injuries. Then she saw me. Her eyes bulged.

Mr. Jackson pointed and growled, "What is he doing here?"

I tried to cower behind Lucy but it was no use. I was taller than she was. *Go on, Lucy*, I thought. *Explain how you scared me into coming here and wouldn't let me leave.*

"Dad," Lucy started, but she was talking to their backs as they entered their house. The police officer herded Lucy and me in behind them.

Everyone was gone. What was left behind looked like the whole house had been turned upside down, shaken violently, and then plopped down without any care.

"Oh, my god. What the hell happened in here?" Mr. Jackson asked. His voice held anger mixed with a big dose of extreme disappointment. It was a sound I knew all too well. As was what came next. His attention turned back toward me. Even Mr. Jackson didn't have any sympathy left for me. "Is he responsible for all of this?"

Before Lucy could jump to my rescue, Mrs. Jackson pointed and barked, "Officer, this boy was told to never step foot in this house again. I want him charged with trespassing!"

I stammered out an unconvincing, "But — No — I —"

"Charge him!" Mr. Jackson demanded.

"Now, hold on," the police officer said. "We'll get there. First things first — we were called here because of a noise issue."

"Mom!" Lucy shouted. "This isn't Tyler's fault."

"Always ready to defend him, huh?" her mother scoffed. "He's not some rescue dog that you can mend. You need to start protecting yourself from people like him, Lucy."

"He's not a dog!"

"So I take it you didn't break up with him?"

I couldn't just stand and watch the fireworks between mother and daughter. I couldn't take it. I wasn't going to cause this family any more trouble. "Shut up!" I yelled. "I'm right here. Lucy is an incredible person and my best friend. I know that I don't deserve her. So charge me. Put me in jail. I don't care anymore!"

My detonation caused a ripple effect. Mr. and Mrs. Jackson were speechless at my admitting to everything they thought of me. The police officer had a look of irritation that she'd been drawn into this mess by a seemingly simple call in.

And just as I publicly sank my relationship with Lucy, Brandon caught everyone's attention.

He staggered out of the kitchen.

The officer took out her pad of paper. "Who is this?"

Even at a distance it was easy to see that Brandon was confused.

The Jacksons rushed to his side.

Mrs. Jackson gasped, "Brandon, dear, what happened to you?"

Brandon was seriously spaced out and couldn't respond coherently. So he tried for casual. "Hey, guys! What's doing?"

His dad held him by the shoulders and looked him squarely in the face. "What have you been drinking?"

The police officer picked up a bottle from the ground and held it out. "I don't think it's what he's been drinking as much as it is what he's been swallowing." She sat Brandon down and kneeled next to him.

Mr. Jackson held up the bottle of pills and read the label. "Where did these come from?"

"Those pills are opioids," said the police officer. "Fentanyl. Pain meds." She shone her flashlight in Brandon's face. "And I bet they were stolen from the person they were prescribed to." She spoke into her walkie talkie, calling for an ambulance. "Your son needs to be checked out and cleared at the hospital. Then we can sort out what the drugs are doing here."

Mrs. Jackson sat at Brandon's side and held his hand. "Lucy, get your brother a glass of water."

Mr. Jackson turned in my direction and came at me, murmuring under his breath. "How can you come here after what we talked about? We made it perfectly clear that you were to stay away."

"Lucy, get your brother a glass of water!"

Then Mr. Jackson aimed his attention at Lucy. "Did you invite Tyler here?"

No way is she taking the blame for me, I thought. "All right! It was me!" I blurted. "I heard there was a party. I figured you guys were away for the night and I showed up to party!"

Mr. Jackson took the bottle of pills. "So this is yours? You brought this into my house?"

I quickly realized that my bravery and care for Lucy had painted me into a very bad corner.

I was trapped. I'd take the trespassing charges, no problem. But I wasn't going to take the blame for throwing the party. And for sure not for stealing someone's painkillers and bringing them here.

"I asked you a question," Mr. Jackson demanded.

"Mr. Jackson, I'd never do anything like that to Lucy or Brandon."

My answer didn't satisfy him, so he pressed on. This time he got close to Brandon. He quietly asked, "Son, who threw this party? Who messed up our house?"

Brandon looked up at his dad. He paused for an amount of time that seemed to stretch into minutes. And then he pointed at me.

I stepped back. "What? No!"

Lucy yelled, "Brandon is lying!"

Mr. Jackson held up his hands to stop us from talking. He leaned close to Brandon again and calmly asked, "Where did you get the pills?"

Brandon took in the question and pointed at me again.

The situation went from explosive to nuclear.

"You did this!" Mrs. Jackson called out, crying. "Tyler Frye, you did this to Brandon!"

I couldn't believe how quick she was to blame me. How quick she was to believe Brandon. Wasn't it obvious he was lying to cover up what he had done?

The police officer turned to me and I had, for a fleeting second, a dark and disturbing thought. At least going to jail would solve my food and housing issues.

Soon an ambulance arrived, adding to the emergency light show. Two medics attended to Brandon. While the medics checked Brandon's vitals, the Jacksons kept on eye on me. If anything happened to their son, they'd be ready to charge me with that too.

I followed the family, the police officer, and the medics outside. It was hard to watch

Brandon on the stretcher as he was placed in the back of the ambulance. This was all too real. Seeing Lucy's tearful reaction made me feel horrible, even though I hadn't done anything to cause this. I was the one trying to help her stop the party.

Mrs. Jackson stepped into the ambulance next to Brandon and it carried them away.

I wondered if they were going to Victoria General. Was my dad working tonight? That would just be too strange.

Mr. Jackson immediately turned to the officer. He pointed at me and said, "I want this boy arrested."

Chapter 12

Anywhere But Home

The officer told me to wait by her cruiser while she had a chat with Mr. Jackson.

Lucy gave me a feeble wave. She mouthed, "I'm sorry," before slipping into the house.

Then the back door of the cruiser was opened and I was invited to sit. My first reaction to being in the back of a cop car was that it was very confining. I felt trapped, like an animal in a cage. The door was shut and the police cruiser pulled away. I caught one last glimpse of the Jackson house through the dirty back window. The car merged onto a main street and I stewed restlessly in the back seat.

I should never have stayed at the house. All of this was totally avoidable. How did I get into a situation like this? Now the officer had all my information and I was officially in the system.

The radio squawked as the officer spoke into it.

I spoke through the wire mesh and Plexiglas that kept me separated from her. "Excuse me. Are you taking me to jail?"

"Is that where you want to go?"

I paused. How honest did I want to be with her? "Actually, maybe. Do I have a choice?"

She chuckled. "Trust me. You don't want to go to jail." She made a turn at a stop sign and continued, "What you allegedly did was not good. But you're not going to jail."

"Oh."

"If I find you were using, pushing, or popping those pills in any way, that's another story. You'll find yourself with a criminal record for breaking and entering and possession." She stopped at a red light.

"Then where are we going?" I asked.

"I'm taking you where you should be — home."

"I'd prefer you took me to jail."

She looked at me quizzically through the rear-view mirror. "You what?"

"I'd rather not go home. Personal reasons." She didn't respond so I added, "Please."

"Unfortunately, kid, you don't have a choice. What's up at home?"

I figured she'd drop me off at the door. If my dad was working, there was no way my mom would answer. Maybe the nurse, but then I could just take off. But if my dad was home . . . "Nothing."

The officer asked, "Then why don't you want to go home?"

I wondered, *Is this my moment? Can I open up to a police officer? Would she understand?*

"Usual stuff," I joked. "My dad likes the Seahawks and I like the Rams."

"So there's an issue with your dad?" After a long moment of silence, the officer offered, "Opioids are a big problem."

"Is that what those were?"

She glanced at me again through the rear-view mirror. "Pain meds."

"Oh."

"They are crazy addictive and deadly if you take too much. Nothing good ever comes from those. Especially fentanyl. It always ends up ruining lives and stealing promising futures away from people, especially teens. That kid's parents need to take him to an addiction clinic."

"I've never touched that stuff. I don't smoke or anything. Not even those e-cigarettes. Vapes."

"That family doesn't seem to think that's the case. And if you were anywhere near the home of the person on that pill label, I'm going to find out."

I came to the quick decision that I should

stop talking to the officer so I didn't incriminate myself in any way.

Soon, my house came into view. The cruiser came to a stop on the driveway. The officer let me out of the car and I did the long, scary walk to the front door.

The officer rang the bell. At first it seemed like no one was home. Then a figure came to the door. I could tell right away from the blurred image through the frosted glass that it was Dad.

The door opened slowly. I'm sure the first thing Dad noticed was the police cruiser on his driveway. The neighbours would be in the know and word would spread like wildfire.

What a moment for my dad. His eyes said it all. His son showing up with a police officer at his side.

My life was full of curveballs and strikeouts, but I never could've predicted this moment. Not in a hundred years. This moment would prove him right. Everything he said and thought about me was true. Skip the trial. Just convict and sentence me.

"Oh, Dr. Frye, from the ER," the police officer started. "I didn't make the connection."

That was it for me. The cop was another fan of the good doctor.

My dad smiled and offered a handshake. "Evening, officer. What's going on here?"

"Your son was found at the Jacksons' house. Apparently trespassing. And someone says he was handing out opioids at a party."

Dad let out a long steady breath and even angled away for a moment. "I see. Did any of those pain medications have my name as prescribing physician?"

"Not that I'm aware of."

"I thought Tyler might have stolen one of my prescription pads." I was shocked at the very idea. But Dad went on, "I thought he knew better than to do something like this." It was like I wasn't even there. "I guess I'm the fool for believing in him. Do me a favour."

The officer nodded. "Yes?"

"Please don't tell anyone about this, unless you absolutely have to."

That's my dad, I thought. The only thing he cared about was his reputation.

"This is very embarrassing for both Tyler and myself," Dad explained to the cop. "I don't want this to become common gossip, if it hasn't started already. My son is a really troubled kid and clearly this will affect his future one way or another. He's got a lot of growing up to do."

The officer clearly thought she was deep in a family moment. "Of course," she said. "If that's all, I'll be heading out."

My dad shook her hand again. "Thank you for bringing him home safely."

I was free of the cop car, but I felt like my hands were tied. The front door was open, but there was no getting out of this one. I stepped inside the house.

Chapter 13

The Big Fight

I was halfway up the stairs by the time I heard the front door close. It was like I was vacuum sealed inside the house. At the top of the stairs I paused. I wanted to see my mother. Her bedroom door was open. But I chose the other direction, toward my bedroom. I closed the door behind me, wishing I could lock Dad out the same way he locked me in.

My bed was made and the school books on my desk were piled neatly next to my computer. I hadn't been online in ages, so none of my social media profiles were active. Did people think I fell off the earth? Maybe they just assumed that I had died.

I flipped open my computer. The screen lit up, but it couldn't connect. I tried the password, but it didn't work. My dad must've changed it or cancelled my account. After debating whether I could sneak into the bathroom and take a shower, I settled on just a change of clothes.

My clean bed called to me. I couldn't resist the temptation of the comfortable mattress and the pull of cool, billowy pillows. I tested the waters with just my hands, for fear of getting too comfortable. I muttered to myself, "Live in the moment," and flopped down onto my bed. It embraced me. It felt like home. I piled my pillows high and let my cheeks absorb the fresh coolness in each of them. I pulled a warm blanket over me. Then I folded my favourite pillow under my head and closed my eyes.

My room was quiet and calm compared to the night I had just had. I couldn't fully process what had gone down. When I thought about Lucy calling me over, the wild party, and Brandon, it seemed like it happened to someone else.

And I had seen enough of the police to last a lifetime.

My eyes were closed, but I wasn't at rest. Too many unanswered questions floated in my mind. Where did Brandon get the drugs? How could I prove that I didn't steal them? That I didn't bring them to the party? If that officer was going to go back and investigate, I couldn't think of anyone who would support me. No one would have anything nice to say about me. The only person on my side was Lucy, but they would claim her viewpoint was tainted.

Soon my questions began to clump together into a giant unsolvable tangle. I had almost forgotten where I was. I was in his house. I needed to get up and get out. I wanted to stick to my plan, but I didn't realize how much I missed my bedroom. The private, quiet, warm space finally won out and I found myself letting go.

***

A strange noise woke me up. I opened my eyes and wiped drool from my lip. I was disappointed that I was still home, flat out on my bed. There was that sound again. I flipped over and saw my dad at the door.

"Comfortable?" My dad swirled his drink.

As I sat up, I identified the sound as the crushed ice in his drink sliding against the glass.

"You've had quite the night, Tyler. A brand-new low for you."

I shot up and started to make the bed. I made sure to remove any imprint I had made.

Dad took a sip that left behind a smirk on his face. "You're falling apart, Tyler. You should know that I've received many calls from your teachers. Let's see . . ." He pressed his glass in his right hand against his bent index finger. "First calls were about missing assignments. Yeah, there were a bunch of those." He took another sip and pushed the glass against his middle finger. "Second came the calls from the guidance department. I guess they were following up. I really didn't know what to say."

I stood still.

"Forget medical school," he chuckled, "you may not pass grade eleven! What do you have to say about that?"

I tried to respond. But my brain couldn't collect the waterfall of words crashing down.

"That's what I thought." He paused for a sip. "Everything I gave you, like this computer —" he knocked it to the floor. "— you throw away. You embarrass me. You embarrass your poor mother."

With each sentence his sips grew, becoming bigger slurps, each followed by a step closer to me. I had been around for many of his benders. But I could tell this one was headed in a dangerous direction.

"You know your mother isn't well. She doesn't need this sort of attention."

His words grew louder and angrier.

"And whether you want to believe it or not, young man, people respect me. Yeah, they do. They look up to me."

His words became slurred from the drink at the same time he stepped into my personal space.

"Do you realize how that looks? My only son failing at school, sleeping anywhere he can find a bed, running all over town like a complete lunatic?"

He tilted and leaned into my face. His wet lips glimmered with the sheen of his drink. I could smell the deep, toxic smell from his glass.

"And those bad choices cast a shadow on your mother and me."

Now he was repeating himself.

"I've given you every chance for success. What else do you want from me, Tyler?"

I said nothing, hoping not to trigger him to violence.

"You've got nothing." My dad looked down like he almost forgot he had a drink in his hand. And then he threw the glass against the wall behind me. The glass shattered across the floor.

I took a deep breath and exhaled.

He looked at me as squarely as he could.

I had to say something. He forced it out of me. "You say I let you down. All you care about is people believing that Mom is sick! But I know that you're keeping her controlled to keep her problems hidden. Dad, Mom has a mental health problem. No one would blame you. But she needs a doctor who can help her, not just keep her drugged!"

"You don't know what you're talking about."

There was no getting through to him. I could no longer believe what he said or care what he felt about me. No matter what I did, it wasn't right because I was me, not him. "You know what else I see, Dad?"

He glared at me.

Tears of fear started to roll down my cheeks. My voice cracked. "I see a drunk."

His eyes went wide. He pointed and shouted, "Get the hell out of here! Get out and don't ever come back!"

I brushed past him and down the stairs. Unsteady on his feet, he was slow to follow me. I could hear him stumbling down the stairs after me. It didn't matter. I slammed the door shut and was gone.

Chapter 14

Shelter

Steady beads of rain mixed with tears had blurred my vision. I wiped the water from my eyes, but they filled up again. I splashed along the darkened sidewalk, my head angled down to cut off the rain.

Tonight sealed my fate. My home was no longer where I lived. Everything I once had was taken by my father. It wasn't just a closed door. I finally reached a break in the downpour when I stepped into the bus shelter.

I sat on the cold bench. The world around me was speckled as water droplets hit and slithered down the glass walls.

Cars sped by with a wet swoosh, but there was no sign of a bus. It was a long ride, but I needed to get downtown to that shelter. I was out of choices. I couldn't burden another friend, another unsuspecting classmate.

A bus finally came into view. It stopped and its doors opened. I took out my transit pass and swiped it. Nothing happened. I swiped it again. Nothing.

The bus driver looked at me and shrugged.

I sighed. My father must've cancelled my pass too.

Getting to the youth shelter was no longer an option. I was stuck in a very different kind of shelter.

After a long time of sitting and zoning out, I couldn't take the discomfort anymore. I tried lying on the metal bench but I kept sliding off. There were three closed corners in the bus shelter. I chose the one in front, furthest away from the wind and rain coming in the entrance.

The cement was even colder than the metal bench. I sat and leaned against the glass wall. My eyes started to close and I felt myself slowly sliding down.

My soft bed with cool pillows and a warm blanket was just a speckled dream.

***

My eyes cracked open just enough to reveal a view I couldn't place. I lifted my head and winced at a series of sharp pains in various parts of my body.

I had fallen asleep on the cold, hard ground. My neck was rigid and a headache slowly festered. My fingertips were numb from the cold and my back felt knotted.

I got to my knees, then used the metal bench to prop myself up. It took a while to collect my thoughts. There was still so much swirling around from what had gone down the day before.

The outside world started to come into focus. I noticed the disturbed look on the faces of two women waiting for the bus. They stood outside the shelter. They were disgusted enough by me to wait outside in the rain. Did they guess that I was a trespassing, pill-dispensing, waste of space?

I cowered back when they started to move toward the opening.

The women entered the shelter and brushed the rain from their coats. I was surprised that they came anywhere near me. Were they going to call the police?

One of them stepped a little closer and said, "Hi."

I didn't respond.

"You don't look old enough to be here alone. Are you in high school?"

They stood side by side and the other

one said, "Is there anything we can do to help you?" She extended her cell phone to me. "Would you like to call someone to come get you?"

I offered a broken smile and pulled my cell phone from my jeans pocket. I held it up, offering it as proof that I was one of them, or at least I used to be.

They looked at me, but the looks on their faces didn't change. I glanced at my phone and saw in the top left corner — *no service*. Dad had dropped me from his data plan.

One of them opened her bag and took out some money.

I held my hand up and shook my head again. I wasn't a beggar.

They gave me a five-dollar bill. As I took it, I thought, *If they only knew who my dad is.*

I folded the money into my pocket and stared at the notice on my phone. Then the battery warning lit up and my phone died. I could see my reflection in the black surface and

I gasped at the image of the dirty version of me. I really could have used one of Brandon's happy pills.

We all turned to the sound of a rumbling bus. I was saved from their generosity and their pity.

I was slow to get to my feet. The world around me was blurry and I felt dizzy. I leaned against a wall. I needed food.

After a few moments I cleared out of the shelter, afraid that I'd stick in the women's hearts enough for them to call the police to rescue me. I needed to get off this island. As I tottered down the sidewalk, it took a coughing fit to clear my roughened chest, clogged from sleeping outside. Aimless at first, I finally clued in to what I needed. And what I needed was at school.

Chapter 15

Abandoned

I rounded the corner toward the high school and saw that the parking lot was empty. Either my timing was way off or it was the weekend. Without my phone, I had no way of knowing. I found a spot to sit and waited until I saw teachers' cars pulling in.

I wondered what Dad had said to them when they called about my missing work. I'd have taken a fail, but that probably wouldn't have stopped them from calling home.

A silver sedan pulled up to the drop-off area. I made out Mr. Jackson behind the wheel. Lucy stepped out and I waited for her to clear the area. Inside the school and down a hallway I found her at her locker.

I approached cautiously so as to not alarm her.

She did a double take when she saw me. "Tyler."

Her reaction confirmed how bad I looked.

I thought about my first words to her. I didn't want to come off desperate or needy, even though I knew I looked it. I only wanted to be near someone who was on my side. She knew the truth.

Her eyes were puffy. Probably from a lack of sleep and crying. I decided to start by asking her how Brandon was doing.

She looked eager to talk about anything but me. "He's home from the hospital and back to normal. Brandon thinks he's invincible. He'd have another party tomorrow if he could."

There was a moment of silence between us. I broke it with, "So your parents really hate me."

"I tried to explain it to them, that it wasn't your fault. But they are convinced that innocent Brandon could never do anything like that."

"Must be nice to have that kind of trust."

Another beat of awkward silence seeped between us.

"Well, it's important to me that *you* know the truth," I finally said. I searched for a smile on her face or the way she always tucked her hair behind her ears, but I got no response I could read.

"I'm sorry, Tyler," she said. "I should never have called you last night."

"Can we talk about something else?"

"Things at home are out of control. My mother blames me too. She thought you and I broke up."

I guess we can't, I thought.

"Now she's watching every move I make. Tyler, we need to cool things for a few weeks."

"I figured you might say something like that. I don't have a few weeks."

"What's that supposed to mean?"

"I mean, I only spent one night on the street and I don't know how much longer I can take that. And I can't keep showing up to school looking and smelling like a bum."

"As sorry as I am that you're going through that, I don't know what to do to help you anymore."

"You can't, Lucy. I get it."

"You're not the same guy anymore, Tyler. We don't talk, hang out, or anything normal like that."

I nodded.

"We never have time alone. We don't do things that normal boyfriends and girlfriends do." She paused as people walked by. "And with the pressure from my parents and you being, well, homeless, I guess I have to break up with you. But I feel like we already broke up a while ago."

I smiled flatly to cover the pain from facing the truth I felt. I wanted to ask her if it was her mom behind this, but I knew this time it was all Lucy.

"Take care of yourself, Tyler." Lucy broke eye contact, but I held on. Waiting, hoping. But it never returned. The cold, awkward silence sliced through me.

A group of girls passed by in a bubble of high-pitched laughter.

Lucy took her binders and said, "I have to go."

As she walked away, I thumped my head against a nearby locker. It was really over.

I headed for the boys' restroom on the second floor where it was quieter and there was less chance of it being used this early. I needed to be alone. It was an added bonus to be inside four solid walls and a roof. I wasn't mad at Lucy. I didn't even have the energy to be mad at my dad.

I made the mistake of turning to the mirror. I looked even worse than my reflection in my dead phone and in Lucy's eyes. The warm water made me feel better but it did nothing for my appearance. I ventured back out into the hallway. Down on the first floor I edged my way into line at the cafeteria. It seemed that the whole school was there waiting for their morning sugar fix. Some people in line covered their noses and mouths in reaction to my smell, but I didn't care. Food was a priority.

I shoved my hand into a basket of granola bars. I one-handed a couple and buried them in my pocket. The line took the smallest of steps forward and I waited for my chance to bail.

I wasn't proud of stealing food. Not even close. But I figured this was my school. I didn't have an overdue library book and used to show up to most sporting events. This time around, it could be here for me.

I got my cue to leave when some kids in line started talking about Brandon's epic party.

I offered an empty, "Excuse me," and a "coming through," before making a sharp turn out of line and into the hallway. I downed my first granola bar, barely taking the wrapper off. I chewed on it not for flavour but for sustenance.

The tiny hit of sugar and carbs cleared my head a bit. I realized that I hadn't decided whether I was staying in school or not. I was tossing the pros and cons around in my head when I heard someone call my name.

Chapter 16

Survival

"Tyler." It was Simon. "You okay?"

"I'd be a lot better if you bought me a coffee and a muffin."

He laughed and then abruptly stopped. "Oh. You're serious."

I offered a nod and a direct smile. At this point, why would I not ask for what I wanted? I needed to be a lot less shy and a lot more obnoxious.

"Uh, okay," Simon said.

I opened my second granola bar, shoved it in my mouth, and then handed him the two wrappers. I held out my index finger while swallowing the bar nearly whole. "And more of these too."

He looked at me, his face full of judgement.

"I'll get you back." I smiled wide. "Promise." As Simon entered the line-up, I called out, "Two sugars!" I felt a lot better not being a thief.

When Simon returned with the goods, I jumped on the muffin. Still chewing, I blew steadily on the coffee until it was drinkable. "Do you see these real chocolate chunks? Who thought caf food could be so good."

Simon laughed. "I'm glad you're happy. You should write an online review."

I laughed, but my focus was on my coffee. A couple sips of the dark stuff and the overnight aches and pains began to fade. "Seriously, Simon. Thank you for this."

"No problem. And you don't owe me anything."

"You sure?"

"Whatever you want. It's hard seeing you like this, man."

"You have no idea what I've been through the last twenty-four hours."

"Tell me."

I didn't know where to start. There was the party, Brandon, the police, my dad, and Lucy. I gave him the short version.

"You're kidding me!" he exclaimed when I had finished. "The police?"

"Yep. And it's even worse than I'm telling you."

"They're investigating you?"

"Yes." I finished off the coffee. "I have no one on my side. Not a single person believes me." I could see Simon putting the pieces of my puzzle together.

"But you said Lucy called you?"

"She broke up with me."

"What?"

"I don't blame her. It makes sense. My life is literally crumbling around me. I was working with Jeffrey, my lab partner, before everything exploded. He told me about getting emancipated. Have you heard of that?"

"Yeah. I know what that is."

Of course he did. Simon was a genius.

"You going to do that, you think?"

"Yeah! That way my dad will have no control over me."

"Neither will your mom."

Simon was always technical. He liked to take anything apart to figure out how it worked. So that's what he was doing with my half-formed plan.

"Yes, you're right. That's the bad part. But I have to try it. Oh, are you ready for some bigger news?"

Simon offered an uncertain nod. "I'm not sure I can handle more."

"I'm leaving Victoria."

"What?"

"I'm getting out. What do I have here?"

It took Simon a long time to say, "Me."

"Sorry, dude, but that's not enough."

"I know. Where would you go?"

"Not a clue. Anywhere as long as it's not here."

Simon lowered his voice. "You can't leave town if the police are investigating you."

"Everyone thinks I'm guilty anyway. So I'm just going to disappear. It'll make everyone involved happy."

Simon shook his head. "Is there another option?"

"I've thought about them all. But I'll admit that I can't think too clearly these days. Is there something different you can see?"

Simon shrugged.

"You're the smartest person I know, Simon. If you can't see a way out of this, then there is no way out."

Simon flapped his hands down in frustration.

"Simon, just one more favour."

"Other than coffee and muffins?"

I gave him my most serious face.

"Joking. Yeah?"

"Don't talk about me. And unfriend me in every possible way."

"What? Tyler! You're my best friend! How do I do that?"

"Like you said. There's an investigation. So when I'm gone, they're going to talk to people to see what happened to me. I don't want you questioned or connected to me."

"But everyone knows we're friends!"

I spoke clearly and directly. "Are you my friend?"

Simon paused, confused by my question. "That's what I just said."

"Then do that."

"Actually, an idea just came to me," Simon offered.

I knew Simon would do anything to get me to stay. But I figured I'd listen. It would be good if he wouldn't be forced into lying to the police about not knowing me. "Go ahead," I said.

He cleared his throat. "Jeffrey."

"What?"

"Before you leave the island, why don't we meet up with Jeffrey? We could learn more about getting you emancipated. And maybe he might see some other options."

I shook my head. "The only option is me off this island."

"Okay then, I'll talk to my mom again. I'll get her to help you."

"No."

"Then let's go to your dad. Together."

"Simon, you're my only friend. Be careful what you're about to say."

"I don't know, Tyler. Maybe we can let him have it. Tell him how it's going to be. Or you find a way to never see each other. You slip in late to sleep and get out before he wakes."

"Hell, no! You think I haven't tried those things? It would only make things worse."

"I guess I'm doing a bad job at trying to help."

"You think you know my dad, but you haven't seen him in a long time. You haven't been around when he's drinking."

"Last time I remember being at your house was for your tenth birthday party."

I remembered that party. My mom was a mom back then. She baked me a cake decorated like a baseball diamond. Simon and a couple other friends slept over. We watched movies and, at that sleepover, we didn't sleep at all. When my mom started getting bad, the only person I'd have over was Simon. Then my dad started getting bad and I kept everyone away.

The bell rang for the start of class.

Chapter 17

Standoff

"Aren't you coming to Science?" Simon asked.

"I haven't decided." Students swarmed around me on their way to class. I sighed and said, "I'm coming."

But then I spotted someone coming at me through the crowd. I had to look twice. But there was that smirk and the stench of that attitude.

"Just keep moving," Simon suggested.

I had a major headache from lack of

food and sleep. Brandon was the last thing I needed.

I cut through the crowd, but Brandon stayed on me. *What does he want from me?* I wondered. Did he need to point out how much I smelled and nail me for what happened with Lucy?

"Hey, jerk!" Brandon called out.

I kept walking, but my frustration was growing. All I ever did was take garbage from my dad and people like Brandon. They pushed me around with their words. They treated me like I wasn't human. Like I didn't have feelings.

"You hear me, jerk?"

His friends were chuckling.

I wanted to make it stop. I wanted everything to stop. So I hit the brakes and turned to face him.

"Bad idea, Tyler," Simon warned.

I pushed toward Brandon. What could he do to me that my dad hadn't already done? Yell at me? Call me stupid? Beat me up? I got in his face and asked, "Do you have any idea what you've done, you moron?"

"Look who it is," he crowed. "The asshat who got dumped by my sister."

Brandon's friends stepped in, but he waved them back. He had to make the performance good for his friends and anyone else in earshot. "It's okay, guys. I can handle this loser."

"Brandon, I'm not taking the fall for your problems," I told him.

"And I'm never coming clean . . . so, that's exactly what you're going to do. And if they don't throw your ass in jail, you can go slime back into whatever hole you crawled out from."

I didn't have a hole to go into. I had nothing.

He spoke loudly for the crowd. "Because you're the one who brought drugs to my party. And everyone you see around me is a witness."

The more he talked the worse my headache got. I needed food, not a fight. It was like every time I went home. I just wanted to eat and go to my room. But when Dad got home and started drinking, he was itching for a fight. And I was the easy target.

"Tell everyone, Tyler, who is your witness?"

"Your sister."

"Really? My parents have her under control. She's never speaking with you again!"

I snarled, "Drug addict."

He hit back with, "Asshat."

"You'd be dead if it wasn't for me, Brandon."

"And you'd be laid if it wasn't for me." That got a howl of laughter from his buddies.

I clenched my jaw. "Joking at your sister's expense? Nice."

I looked around and noticed that the crowd had doubled in size. And with each insult, Brandon got more and more approval from the crowd.

"At least I have friends to back me up."

"They're not your friends if they're there to wreck your house."

"How would you know? You have no friends. Unless you count that Asian geek over there."

That got some *oohs* from the crowd. They started jostling Simon. I needed to end this before it got uglier. I drew back my right arm, clenched my fist and punched Brandon in the face.

Brandon recoiled backward as pain rushed through my hand. But he recovered quickly and slammed me with a blow to the side of my face. My world went quiet for a moment. Then Brandon jumped on me and took me down to the ground.

The crowd boiled over in excitement.

I tried to swat Brandon away, but he had the advantage. I kicked up with my knees a few times and he finally rolled over. Then I felt a strong pull.

"Break it up!"

A teacher yanked me to my feet and away from Brandon.

Brandon snarled at me. "I'm going to tell the police you assaulted me!" He spoke in a low voice so no one else could hear.

"What was that all about?" the teacher asked.

"Oh, it's nothing," Brandon said. "We know each other really well. We weren't really fighting."

"Didn't look that way." Doubt clouded the teacher's face.

"It was a family feud," I said. "I used to date his sister."

The teacher looked at me. After a moment he nodded like he got it. He gave me a tap on the shoulder and a stern warning. He ordered me to go to class.

Simon was quick to catch up with me. He looked at me with a certain amount of shock and a whole lot of amazement. "Wow, dude. Who the hell are you and what did you do with my friend?"

"Brandon is framing me for something I didn't do. And it looks like he's going to get away with it!"

Simon punched at the air. "But you really let him have it!"

I shrugged.

"But Brandon hates that you got the better of him. He's going to come back at you with his friends."

I stopped. "Thanks for the heads up, I guess. Why does everyone believe him? He's a superficial, drugged-up loser."

"How are you going to prove that he got the drugs?"

"I don't think I can. And I really haven't had time to think about that."

"You could beat the truth out of him."

I smirked. "Yeah, if I had a death wish. It's just as well I'm leaving for good."

It was decided. I was leaving. I just had one stop to make first.

Chapter 18

Farewell

As I approached the house a tidal wave of
memories flooded my brain. I shook them
out of my head to double and triple check
that Dad's car was not in the driveway. Then
I peered in the windows, looking for any sign
of movement. I reached for the door handle
and inserted my key in the front door. I was
surprised it still worked. I guess Dad hadn't had
time to change the locks yet.

I stepped into the house, keeping an eye

out for the nurse. She wasn't there, and the house was completely quiet. But I still felt like eyes were on me.

First stop was my bedroom. I grabbed my school backpack, emptied out what I didn't need and then stuffed it with clothes. I moved through my room, ignoring all my favourite possessions. It was the only way I could pull this move off. Then in the bathroom I grabbed my toothbrush, toothpaste, and deodorant. I never thought I'd miss these items most of all.

I couldn't get the backpack closed, but I didn't care. I dragged it into the hallway and placed it at the top of the stairs. I stood there, listening for any sign of the nurse. Still nothing.

The entrance to my parents' bedroom loomed before me. I slowly pushed open the double doors and stopped at the sight of Mom lying in bed. No nurse. Mom's eyes were closed. The TV was tuned to a shopping channel, but the sound was off.

How could I leave her? What kind of person did that make me? I guessed it meant I was the kind of person Dad thought I was. None of this was Mom's fault, and she would take my leaving really hard. Could I just say goodbye and walk away?

I ordered myself to stay on task. I told myself that, once I got settled somewhere, maybe I could come back and visit her. I stepped closer to her as the carpeted floor muffled any sound of my passing. I coughed twice to announce myself so that I didn't startle her and followed it with, "Mom."

I kneeled beside the bed and gave her a moment to wake up. I put my hand on her duvet, hoping that she'd sense it was me. I said, "Mom," a little louder. She still didn't respond.

The bedside table I was kneeling beside was a mess. Cluttered around her clock and remote control were bottles of pills.

Does she really take all these pills? I wondered.

My mom made a noise like she was slowly waking.

As I scanned the labels on the pill bottles, I saw that Dad's name was listed on every one. And a couple of the drug names stood out. Hydrocodone. Fentanyl. My dad had my mom on heavy-duty painkillers. I slowly extended my arm and reached for a bottle that was nearly full. I thought of how out of it Brandon had been. That might not be such a bad state to be in, and these pills could help me. I couldn't imagine sleeping outside again. But if I did and I had these, maybe it wouldn't be as bad. They'd change my reality. Maybe they'd trick my brain into thinking I was staying at a five-star hotel by the beach. Maybe I could be surfing the waves of the crystal blue water instead of being flat out on the hard, cold, dirty cement ground. Maybe they could make me feel like I was loved.

But if I got hooked on these, I'd be just like my mom. Medicated and managed by my dad. Maybe dead, if what the police officer said was more than just an attempt to scare me straight.

That gave me another idea. Dad may have cut off my allowance, but I could sell Mom's pills to people like Brandon. I'd be smart enough to rip the labels off. It would be ironic if I was making survival money off Dad's prescriptions. It would be just what my dad deserved.

I was slipping one pill bottle in my pocket when I heard my mother's voice call out, "Tyler?"

"Yes. It's me, Mom."

She propped herself up on a pillow. Her hair was a mess and her face had no colour at all. But it was comforting to see her awake.

"How are you, Mom?" I asked gently.

"Oh, just fine. What about you?"

"I'm okay."

She looked at me and it took a second for her to follow her train of thought. "How's school going?"

"Good, Mom. But I'm here to talk about something else."

"And Lucy? Please tell her I say hello."

When was the last time she saw Lucy and me together? I tried to get her to focus. This was more important. "Mom."

"You're lucky to have Lucy. She's such a sweet girl."

"Yes, she is awesome. I will tell her you say hello."

"Thank you. I'm sorry I haven't been available to you. I guess I'm just not myself . . ."

I appreciated her words, but I didn't have time to give my mom a reality check. I was on a mission. Get in and get out before my dad got home. "Mom, I'm going away."

Some of the happiness on Mom's face was wiped away by the thought. "Tyler, what do you mean?"

"I'm leaving Victoria. It might take me a couple years, but I promise that when I get settled, I'll come visit."

The corners of her eyes drooped with sadness. "Couple of years? Where would you go?"

I didn't have a direct answer. "I'll be okay. I promise."

"No, you stay here until you finish high school."

"Mom, this is my choice. It's all good." I could see that she didn't know how to work through my mixed messages. I was sandwiching the truth with thick layers of baloney — that it was all going to be okay. It wasn't, not even remotely close. I knew that, and somewhere in her drug-addled brain, she did too.

"No, no." She looked up at the door and called out for my dad. "Jack!"

Did she have any idea what time it was? What day it was? I rested my hands on her outstretched arms. "Mom, Dad's at work. He'll be back later."

My mom tried calling him again. When there was no response, she leaned back onto her pillows. "Don't go, Tyler. We can talk about it."

My exit was failing and I needed to stop this tailspin. "Okay, Mom, I won't go anywhere."

"There you go. That's my boy. You have a bright future ahead of you."

I gave her a hug and as I turned away, I said, "Love you." She didn't answer because she had already rolled over in bed.

I grabbed my backpack and stopped when I got to the landing. This was a rare chance, I thought, with my dad and the nurse not here. I stepped into Dad's home office. Medical diplomas and awards were plastered all over the walls. I moved toward his pristine oak desk. Everything was neatly in its place. Behind his desk, on a shelf, were some family photos. I reached for one, but had to stop when I thought I heard a noise. I waited, still as a statue, praying that it wasn't my dad. He would flip if he knew I was here.

Finally, when I was sure no one was there, I turned to his desk and started rifling through drawers. I found an envelope with cash. Not a lot, but more than the nothing I had in my empty wallet. I took half of it and left.

Chapter 19

No Shelter

I hurried out the door. With each step, I was putting more distance between myself and my dad. I got to the end of the driveway and suddenly stopped.

The emotions I bolted down were coming loose and surfacing. When the anxiety hit, I started to run. I was in a full-on sprint. My backpack jolted up and down, jamming into my back with each stride. I raced to a park I used to ride my bike in when I was a little kid.

I pushed past a soccer field and made my way to a treed area. *I can be alone here*, I thought. I zigzagged between trees and came out on a winding bike path. I followed it toward the water's side where I dumped my backpack on a park bench. I squatted down low like I was taking cover from an explosion. And that's where I came undone.

Images of my mother and father flashed through my mind like bolts of lightning. Tears flowed over my face like a downpour. I just let it out, whimpering and cowering. My lungs heaved for air, as I struggled against the storm of emotion.

The tears slowly dried and my breathing returned to normal. I turned to the vast, open water. The sky might have been clouded, but the white-capped, choppy water was still a striking shade of blue. Then something in the distance caught my eye. It was a boat. As my eyes gained focus, I could make out its shape. It was a ferry. It was a beacon calling me from afar, showing me my way off this island.

***

My eyes popped open in panic. I frantically searched for a landmark to place my location. I looked up and saw two dark wood planks. I blinked repeatedly to clear my eyes. I just spent the night under a park bench.

Elbows tucked, I rolled out and got to my feet. The clouds had cleared and the water looked calm. I gazed out at it a moment before pulling my backpack from under the bench. The pack had a sizeable dent where I had used it as a pillow. I stretched out the parts of me that had been in contact with the hard ground.

I dared to wonder for a split second if my mom would report my visit to my dad. Then I pushed the wasteful wonder out of my mind and was on the move.

I walked with purpose, checking that I still had the sixty dollars I had taken from Dad's office. Not much to launch my new life. It might be just enough for a bus and ferry ticket.

After waiting a bit at the bus stop, I realized it was a luxury I could do without. So I started the long walk from Oak Bay to downtown Victoria. With a couple of rests forced by my boulder of a backpack, it took me an hour and change.

The Capital City Station was a transportation hub for the ferry, city buses, and shuttles to the airport. I remembered it well. Five years before, Dad had taken me to a hockey game on the mainland. It was a big deal to go to Vancouver and see the Canucks play. It was a real guys' trip — we took the ferry and stayed overnight in a nice hotel.

I stepped into the station and approached the kiosk. A woman with a name tag reading *Rita* looked at me and asked what I needed.

"How much is a ferry ticket to Vancouver?" I asked.

"How old are you?"

"Sixteen."

"Shouldn't you be in school?"

She's right, I thought. I ran through possible excuses in my head and chose one at random. "I have a prep."

"So you plan on using your prep period to go to Vancouver and get back to school today? The ferry ride to Vancouver is an hour and a half, plus boarding time."

"Oh." I needed to change my game plan. I recovered with a smile. "The ticket isn't for today. It's for Saturday."

"Tomorrow?"

Without a working phone, I had no idea what day it was. "Yes. Sorry about that. I'm going to visit a friend. How much is it?"

"Fifty dollars and fifty cents."

I held out the sixty dollars I took from Dad's desk. *That didn't last long*, I thought. *Should've taken more!*

I took my change as a printer spat out my ticket. Then Rita spat out a phrase like she'd done it a thousand times. "Detailed information on routes are available on . . ." she pointed without looking ". . . the information board and online. Check crossing times before your arrival as schedules can change without prior notice."

I thanked her and walked outside. I took the fact that I couldn't use my ticket until tomorrow as a sign. Since I was stuck here, I thought maybe I should say goodbye to Simon. I splurged and bought a bus ticket costing two dollars and fifty cents. It would take me back to Oak Bay one last time.

Chapter 20

Set Up

It was lunch period at school and I knew exactly where to find Simon. He was in the library doing his homework.

He looked up and dropped his pencil. "Tyler, where have you been?"

I sat down and showed him my ferry ticket. "Tomorrow, I am out of here. So I thought I'd say goodbye."

"You're really going?"

I nodded. Wasn't the ticket proof enough?

"Where will you go?"

"No idea." I held up my phone. "I'm officially cut off by my dad. No bus pass. No computer. No phone. Thought I could use a school computer to do some research."

"What about all your projects? You're going to miss exams. You'll fail grade eleven."

What I was doing was unthinkable to a guy like Simon. In a way I was glad he lived a life that kept him from getting it. "School is the last thing on my mind, Simon. Remember the police?"

"And you don't think they'll track you down wherever you go? You'll be a fugitive."

"Stop it, Simon. You can't scare me into not going. I've made up my mind."

"You are crazy. You don't know anyone on the mainland. Here you have friends. Here you can turn to people for help."

"Let's see who I have here if I stay. There's my loving dad, who I can always *not* count on. And who else? Oh yeah, the police!" I looked up at some students and regretted saying that so loudly.

"Okay, so let's say you go," Simon started. "You arrive, find some shelter, then what? You can't just show up at a local high school. You need an address that says you can go there."

Simon was a quick thinker and he had a logical counter to anything I threw at him. It was time for a curveball. "Then I won't go to school."

"Tyler, you can't do that."

"I can. If I have to. I'll find a job."

"You are such a smart student. What, are you just going to waste all your potential?"

"You know the rule of three?"

"Yes. 'Three weeks without food, three days without water, and three hours without shelter.'"

"So finding real shelter comes before school. And figuring out what I'm going to do with the rest of my horrible life will take money."

"That rule applies to harsh conditions out in the wild. Not in Victoria or Vancouver. You've been sleeping outside for longer than three hours, right?"

"Look, Simon, I didn't come to debate this. I came to say goodbye."

"Goodbye?"

"Yes." I held out my hand to shake. "Goodbye."

Simon didn't take it. "If you trust me at all as your best friend, let's sit down with Jeffrey and talk about options."

"No thanks. No more talking. I know when I'm not welcome. And this island is no longer my home." I snatched my ticket from Simon's hands in case he had any ideas to rip it up.

"I'm gonna miss you," Simon said sadly.

I nodded. "We can text." Then I remembered my dead phone. "Oh, never mind. Scratch that." I smiled for him. "I promise to visit. I want to come back and see my mom anyway."

"Fine. At least let me walk you out."

"Okay. That sounds like a plan."

"I'll just go throw my books in my locker." Simon saw me eyeing his lunch box. "You can have everything in there. I'll be right back."

Simon left and I jumped on his lunch. I realized that the only place I was going to miss even a little on the island was this school. I plowed through a turkey sandwich and got up. Inhaling a granola bar, I took a piece of paper from the library printer and borrowed a pen from the sign-out desk. I returned to the table to write a quick thank you note I could leave in Simon's lunch box.

The library doors swung open. I turned to see Principal Afari enter. She said, "Tyler, I need you to come with me."

I stood. "What? Why?"

"The police are here. They want to speak with you."

I let her take me out through the library doors, trying to figure out how she knew I was at school today. Then I caught a glimpse of Simon cowering against a wall.

I called out to him, "How could you do this to me?"

He looked back at me sheepishly. The principal must have asked him to notify her if he saw me here. *This is it*, I thought, *I'll never make it out of here.*

Dead man walking, I thought as we made our way down the hallway. Why did I come to school? Why didn't I find a phone and call in my goodbye? In a couple of minutes I'd be facing trespassing, break and entry, and drug possession charges. I could see my dad at my trial. He'd be the prime witness testifying against me. "*Lock him up!*" my dad would say! I gritted my teeth in anger at my stupidity. I was like the bad guy at the end of an action movie. Free to escape, he returns one more time to prove something to himself. I should have taken the money and run.

Principal Afari's high-heeled shoes cleared

the way with a loud *clickety-clack*. I trailed in her wake. And as much as I thought about it, I knew making a run for it was not an option. *You had your chance*, I screamed at myself.

I tried to keep up, my head down to deflect stares from passing students. The way they looked at me, I wondered if they knew something I didn't. Was there a wanted poster with my face on it? Gossip travelled quickly on social media and I had been disconnected from that world long enough that I had no idea. For all I knew, Brandon's version of the truth actually was the truth by now. I was overcome by the gravity of regret. I shouldn't have just accepted the lies placed on me. I should have fought back harder to prove my innocence.

Principal Afari reached to open her office door. I closed my eyes for just a second and took in some short breaths, preparing for the storm. Stepping into her office, I was reminded of the presence of a police officer. He was daunting in his black uniform. Any confidence

I had suddenly drained away. I was deeply scared. If it meant I didn't have to talk to the officer, I would confess and go down for a crime I didn't commit.

Principal Afari introduced him as the school liaison officer. He looked at me from under his brimmed hat. Then he motioned me to sit.

Was I actually thinking that I'd outrun the police and evade them in Vancouver? How crazy and desperate was I? I sank into the chair, my stomach queasy and head dizzy. Then I turned when I sensed someone else in the room.

My father.

Chapter 21

Turnaround

He sat cross-legged on a couch in the corner. He wore dark suit pants, a pressed blue button-down, and shiny black leather shoes. He looked very calm and collected, empty of any emotion at my appearance.

I wanted to plead my case, but my mouth had become dry like sandpaper. Principal Afari leaned over the edge of her desk. Her plum-coloured hijab draped down. "We brought you here to let you know that there was an incident last night. Brandon Jackson overdosed."

"What?" my voice cracked. I was so scared by the police and then my dad, I could barely process the news. "Is Brandon . . . dead?"

"Thankfully, no. His parents found him on his bedroom floor. He had ingested more opioids than his system could handle. He is being treated at the hospital and they expect a full recovery."

I sat back in my seat, relieved to hear that Brandon would be okay. My dad looked at me, still no expression on his face. Why was he here? Were they here to blame me for Brandon's overdose?

"I promise I wasn't near him."

How could I prove my whereabouts? *Please officer, I have an alibi. I was sleeping under a bench.*

Principal Afari stood and put her hand on my shoulder. "It's not like that."

The police officer explained, "Brandon's mother found him in the early morning hours. She called emergency services and brought a pill bottle she found next to him so the hospital doctors would know what he took. Police cross-checked the name on the bottle and connected it to another break-in."

I looked back at them, confused.

The police officer continued. "About an hour ago at the hospital, Brandon came clean to his parents and the police about everything."

"Everything?" I asked.

"Yes. According to the officers on scene, Brandon admitted to lying about you giving him the drugs." The officer closed his notepad. "We are now investigating the break-ins. Apparently, Brandon wasn't alone."

Principal Afari beamed at my dad and then at me. "All charges against you are officially dropped."

The police officer reiterated. "Trespassing, breaking and entering, underage possession. All cleared."

"That's great news, Tyler," Principal Afari exclaimed.

I nodded, but didn't smile.

"She is right, Tyler," the officer said. "I've seen too many scenarios like this one go from bad to worse. But he's going to be okay and you are a free young man."

If this is everything, then okay, I thought. But it wasn't. Not even close. I had bigger fish in the fryer. I glanced at my dad.

He remained motionless.

I think he came expecting the same results as I did. My arrest and fall from grace. This was supposed to be his moment to prove to everyone once and for all what he already knew. That I was a failure. The good doctor's son wasn't a young prodigy. People would know that he tried his best. That it was in no way his fault.

But it didn't turn out that way. Now my dad's cool and calm exterior composure was damaged. He looked genuinely upset to hear my good news. He was probably regretting that he had taken time off work to be here.

"So, what now?" I asked.

The officer said, "If you don't have any

questions for me, then we are all good."

I shook my head no and he patted me on the back before he left.

The three of us were alone in the office — my principal, my dad, and me.

"Well then," Principal Afari started. "Why don't we —"

I cut her off by launching to my feet. "I'm free to go?"

"Yes," she said.

I propelled myself past my dad toward her office door. I took my freedom out the door with me. Gunning for the exit, I reluctantly stopped when Principal Afari called for me. "Tyler." She approached and looked at me with concern. "Is everything okay?"

"That's too big a question."

"Excuse me?"

This was my life. It wasn't some class. Did she want a written response? "I can't answer that."

"You barely reacted to the good news about the charges."

I shrugged.

"And I can't help but notice real tension in the room between you and your father."

Tell me something I don't know, I thought.

"Well, if you ever need to talk, my door is always open."

Too little, too late, I thought. I turned and left as quickly as I was forced to enter. Simon was standing off to the side of the doors to the main office.

I blasted past him. He chased after me, but I took no notice. He followed me to the boys' restroom until I said, "Back off."

Alone in the washroom, I moved to a toilet stall and shut the door behind me. I dug into my backpack and pulled out my mom's pill bottle. I wrenched the top off and stared at the pills. I could keep them in case I needed a little help through the night. I could sell them.

But I knew I didn't want to become numb and needy like my mom. And I couldn't be responsible for hurting another Brandon. I dumped the pills in the toilet and watched them dissolve. Then I ripped the bottle's label off. I scrunched my dad's name and contact info into a little ball and dropped it into the toilet bowl. Then I stayed to watch it all flush away.

Back in the hallway, Simon was waiting for me.

He followed me through the school doors. Out in front of the school I stopped. "What do you want?"

Simon was out of breath. "I'm so sorry, Tyler."

"Okay?" I was mad at him, but not as much as I was mad at everything else.

"I should never have set you up like that. I understand if you don't want to see me again. But you have to know I was trying to help. I am truly sorry."

I reached out my arms and gave him a hug.

His voice was muffled by my shoulder. "I'm confused."

"Me too, Simon."

Chapter 22

Crossroads

Coffee shops were my new favourite hangout.
For a couple of dollars I had a warm cup of
coffee and a place to stay. A chair of my own
and a spot to sit where I didn't feel unwanted.
And it was much more comfortable than a park
bench. I could lean back, linger, and listen in
on other people's talk. It was a great escape,
even for a little while. Some people worked on
their laptops while others just chatted. I looked
on and fantasized about the ordinary.

At the coffee shop there were no dirty stares or accusations of trespassing. Instead, I was accepted as one of them without question. As long as I had a cup of coffee in hand. *This is the kind of rent I can afford to keep paying*, I thought.

As I savoured a sip, an oatmeal cookie in the glass case called to me. *Even a coffee was a sizeable percentage of your life's savings*, I reminded myself. The oatmeal cookie eventually backed down.

I took out the ferry ticket and examined it. I tried to visualize myself on the boat pictured on the ticket. As I stood on the deck, the city of Victoria would slowly slip away below the horizon. I wondered what that would feel like. Would I feel free?

Or would I be even more messed up? I had grown up in Victoria. I had friends and knew where things were. What would my first night in Vancouver be like? I'd be arriving in a big city with nothing and no one. I'd really be a runaway and on the streets. And that scared me.

But I already had the ferry ticket. Should I just go?

I knew the best decision I had made was when I flushed those pills. I didn't want to hurt anyone else. But I also wanted to save myself from a life of break-ins and overdoses.

I was still going back and forth on what to do when the door of the coffee shop chimed open. It revealed Simon and Jeffrey. When they stopped in front of me, I said to Simon, "Looks like you've already found a replacement for me."

Simon grabbed an extra chair and they sat across from me. "You figured us out," Simon grinned. "Looks like you've had a busy day. What happened? Give us the details."

I gave them the full update, including my dad's complete lack of reaction to being wrong about me.

"That's great news!" Simon exclaimed. "Well, not for Brandon. Great for you. Hopefully Brandon will get help with his addiction."

"Yeah," I said. "I'm actually glad for Lucy. She also had to deal with this."

Simon asked, "Have you spoken to her?"

"No. Lucy and I are way done. There was too much drama around me and she needs to focus on school."

"Hold on," Simon started. He counted on his fingers, starting with his thumb. "The Jacksons accused you of trespassing."

"Yep."

"And they accused you of distributing opioids to their son and others at that party."

"Right again."

He tapped his middle finger. "And because of their false claims you were investigated for doing a break and enter to get those drugs."

"Yeah."

Simon wasn't paying attention and went back to his thumb. "And if Brandon didn't overdose you would have been charged and had a record."

"Yes. Thanks for the summary report. Your point is?"

"Don't you want an apology from the Jacksons? Don't you want them to have to come to you and give you a big, juicy public apology?"

"You need to go to law school, Simon. You're very good."

"Thanks. Okay, forget the apology. You are a free person. You don't have to run away."

"Ahh, you're forgetting about my dad."

"He's just one person," Simon said. "You run away and he wins."

I gestured at Jeffrey. "I'm happy to see you, but why are both of you here?"

Simon looked a little embarrassed. "I told you that maybe Jeffrey had a way of helping you. So I talked to him and he was happy to come talk to you."

"Took two coffee shops," Jeffrey shifted in his seat, "but we found you. I know you and I are in different situations, Tyler. And I don't want to overstep in any way."

"But?"

"I spoke with my foster parents. They said that you can stay with us for a bit."

I was amazed. Jeffrey and his parents didn't even know me, and they were opening their home to me. "Wow. Thank you, Jeffrey. I really appreciate that."

"You've met them. They are really nice people and they have an extra bedroom."

"You are all so nice to look out for me. I am blown away by how generous everyone is."

"There's a *but* coming," Simon said.

I smiled and dropped the *but.* "*But* I need something more than a short-term solution. I can't couch hop anymore. I really need to figure out what I'm going to do and where I'm going to live. Long term."

The choices continued to bounce back and forth in my head. *Go to Vancouver and fight just to survive . . .*

"So you're going to Vancouver then," Simon stated.

Or stay here and prove to Dad that I'm not a failure.

I revealed the ferry ticket under my palm. "I really want to get off this island, guys," I said, holding it up. "But I'm so tired of running around. And going to Vancouver, to a new city where I don't know anyone — well, that just means even more running around."

Simon did a fist pump in the air. "So you're staying?"

I nodded, even though I wasn't convinced I had made the right choice. For one second, I thought about ripping the ticket in half. It would ensure there was no going back on my decision. But getting a refund and the money back in my hands was more important than a dramatic effect.

Simon and Jeffrey were hanging onto my every word. They were probably grateful not to be in my situation. To not have to make the kind of choices I had to. And I really wished I was telling the story of someone else. But I wasn't. "After everything I've been through, I know that running away won't change my situation."

"So what are you going to do?" Simon asked.

"To start. I'm staying in Victoria."

"You can't do it alone," Jeffrey said. "Trust me, I tried."

"I don't have anyone except you guys."

"Yes, you do," Jeffrey said. "There are social workers who have devoted their lives to helping people like you. People in your situation. They will tell you your options."

"I don't know any social workers."

"Yes, you do," Simon said. "Remember?"

It took me a second to clue into what he was talking about. "Yeah, I remember."

Chapter 23

Unplugged

I reached for the call button by the gate to the shelter. After a moment I heard a buzz and walked through the door that was covered in paint. I recognized the social worker from before. "Wenonah?" I asked.

She smiled. "I remember you. Come on in. Tyler, right?"

"Yes," I nodded. "I need a place to stay."

Wenonah led me inside. "You've come to the right place." Just like last time, people my age were sprawled on benches and on the mismatched couches. Those who were awake barely looked it.

Wenonah lowered her voice. "They're sleeping because they've been up all night on the streets."

I nodded. I felt a connection with them that I didn't have the last time I was there. I could relate to being on the street at night. I now noticed that the benches were padded with cushions. That was a big deal. And I'd take any furniture, no matter how mismatched, for a night anytime.

"I'm glad you gave us another try," said Wenonah. "You know, a lot of people come in, look around, and get scared by what they see."

That was definitely me, I thought.

"Plus there are a lot of stereotypes attached to shelters. Theft, fighting, that kind of stuff. But you won't find that here."

I tried not to say too much or judge other people as Wenonah led me down a hallway into the main area.

"This is an emergency shelter," she explained. "So we do our best not to turn anyone away. If there's space on the couch, it's yours. If there's a spot on the floor, then it's yours." She grabbed a clipboard and pen.

"What's that for?"

"For your intake. I need to take your info so I can get you access to stay here. Tyler, have a seat and relax. Can I get you a drink?"

I shook my head, even though I really wanted something.

"Maybe later then. So I'm going to run through some of the required questions. Please don't feel ashamed. If you think I haven't seen it, I have. If you think I haven't heard it, I have. Good?"

"Yes."

"Have you ever slept on the street?"

"Yes."

"Last night?"

I nodded.

"Have you ever done sex work?"

I tried not to react. That would be showing judgement, and who was I to judge? "No."

"What about drugs or alcohol?"

I thought about what happened to Brandon and what I was accused of. I wanted to laugh. "No."

"Can I see your arms?"

I held them up. Wenonah rolled up my sleeves and examined them. She peppered me with more questions — my age, my gender, what grade I was in — and I did my best to answer them.

"I'm going to run through some more questions. Just stop me if it's a yes or you want to ask something."

"All right."

"Do you have any physical concerns right now?" She looked up at me and then continued. "Do you take any prescription medications? Have you ever been diagnosed with a mental condition?"

My dad might argue with that one, I

thought. All the times he called me crazy and accused me of deliberately hurting him and my mom.

"Have you ever been arrested?"

"Charged. But they were dropped. Does that count?"

"I'll put no. Have you ever been the victim of domestic violence or family violence?"

I shrugged. "Not sure. I've never been hit."

"It's not just that. What about verbal abuse? Have you been threatened?"

Her question triggered a flood of incidents. There were so many times my dad called me useless and stupid. And he threatened me if I didn't, as he liked to say, pull my weight. He locked me in as if I was a wild animal. But if I was being honest with myself, he was the unpredictable one. And when he drank, he frightened me.

"It looks like you're thinking about something. Have you ever been threatened?"

That lumpy feeling in my throat appeared

and my skin felt like it was on fire. I said a quiet, "Yes." Maybe it was saying it out loud to someone, but something in me seemed to break. I fought to hold back tears.

Wenonah put her hand on my shoulder. "Verbal abuse leaves bruises too. They're just harder to see."

I nodded and wiped away a tear. After a moment I asked, "What do you do with that information?"

Wenonah put her clipboard down. "It only goes to central intake. They're the people who work hard to try to find a housing service match for you."

"What kind of housing?"

"It's called transitional housing. It's not an emergency shelter — it's more long term than that. It gives you time to figure things out."

"Okay."

"Tyler, the bad news is that you have to be here. But the good news is that you are a great candidate for transitional housing. Think about it. A real place to stay and call home for a while."

"That would be great. So, what do I have to do while I'm here?"

"This is an emergency shelter so the focus is on your safety. No homework or anything like that."

"That's fine with me," I joked.

"Let's get you something to eat. You can settle in and we'll wash those clothes."

"I have some fresh ones in my backpack that I can change into."

"Doesn't matter. If you've been on the street, we have to run everything through the washer and dryer. Trust me, you don't want to bring bed bugs in here."

It took an hour for me to get cleaned up. In the kitchen, I added hot water to an udon noodle container and stirred it with a spoon. I found an empty spot on the couch and took a blanket from a basket. An old *Mission Impossible* movie was playing on an outdated

TV. The last time I saw that movie, I was home with my parents when everything was normal. They let me stay up beyond my bedtime to watch to the end.

The memory hurt like a punch. I figured that kind of memory might hit me from behind a lot.

I was alone, but at least I wasn't completely alone. The movie played and I couldn't help but wonder what everyone else's story was.

Chapter 24

Changes

I sat in a circle with the other house members. After the emergency shelter, I was lucky to find a spot here. It felt good to be warm and clean and have somewhere to sleep. The house was small and there were sixteen of us squeezed into eight shared rooms. But it was where I needed to be. Surrounded by other teens like me. Our link was the common thread of our troubled pasts.

The house mentor Adrian was a former street kid. He had black cropped hair that matched his skin colour. He told me that each of the tattoos running down his arms were memories of the people he met on the street and in the shelters. He was in the middle of running our weekly meeting. Everyone took turns sharing something positive about their week.

Being the new guy, I was still learning people's names. I was almost too shy to share.

"Tell us about your new school," Adrian prompted.

"It's going okay. I miss my old school, but at least I know some people from here."

My roommate, Will, pointed at me. "That's right, T-man."

I smiled. We were in the same Math class and he always looked out for me. "But it's going well. It has been a while since I've been able to focus on school work and studying. So I'm grateful to have that back."

"Great to hear." Adrian always smiled when he spoke and really listened when people talked.

Adrian continued, "Listen up, everyone, remember to maintain focus and keep up with the routines. Sign in and sign out when you come and go."

I had been locked in my room so many times. I had been forced to sneak in and out of the house that wasn't my home. Signing in and out was okay by me.

"Keep your room and the common space clean. Stick to the curfew. No violations. Follow your individual case plans too."

In my first week, Adrian had sat me down. Together we had created an individual plan for me. It included going to school, getting good grades, and finding something that I was passionate about.

"And of course, this goes without saying, show up at every house meeting. We are successful if we work together."

The group applauded.

"You all get money for attending. So if that's not incentive, I don't know what is!"

There was laughter.

"Oh, and one more thing. Tomorrow night is Sunday, so we are building meals for the week."

At first I was surprised at the support that we got from the community. My dad had always talked about the community as if they were his subjects and he had to be revered as their king. It was totally different here. In my second week a woman working at a big bank came in and talked about financial literacy — how to save money and open a bank account. Then we had a tech guy show us how to computer code. And every Sunday, a real chef came in. We'd go shopping for food, then prep, cook, and clean as a team.

"You all know Franco's, the Italian restaurant on the corner?" Adrian asked.

Almost everyone did.

"I'm excited to tell you that the chef from Franco's is coming to help out. Caesar salad, bruschetta, and pasta."

There were cheers.

I had received compliments from last week's chef and it got me thinking of it as a possible career choice. I liked cooking, and no one ever goes hungry working in a kitchen. Feeding people is as necessary as healing people. And maybe one day, I could pay it forward.

After the meeting ended, I helped stack the chairs. Adrian gave me my meeting money and a reassuring pat on the shoulder on my way out. The floorboards squeaked under me as I moved through the old house. I entered my bedroom. It was smaller than my old one at home, and only half of it was mine. There wasn't much alone time in a shelter like this, but it wasn't like I would trade it in for the streets. I grabbed my jacket and signed out. I had been looking forward to this afternoon all week.

* * *

I strolled the downtown Victoria waterfront. The rain had cleared and it seemed like everyone was out on the streets. I passed the historic Empress hotel, all covered in ivy. Then I stepped onto the busy boardwalk. With the marina and boats to my left, I checked out what the street vendors had to sell. Most were selling keychains, T-shirts, and other Victoria souvenirs.

My favourite vendor was an artist who painted orca whales. They were amazingly life-like and looked happy and confident, jumping out of the water. I thought about saving up my meeting money and buying one for my mom. I really missed her and wanted her to have one in her room. Then when my dad got home, he'd see the new painting and know it was from me. It could be a sign to him that I'm alive and doing okay. Life wasn't perfect, but I could show him I was strong like an orca, the most powerful animal in the ocean.

Halfway down the boardwalk, I found Simon sitting under a tree. I gave him a high-five and a bro hug. "Where's Jeffrey?"

Simon pointed. Jeffrey was trying to gain control of a melting ice cream cone. He waved and walked over.

"How's the old neighbourhood?" I asked.

"Nothing's changed," Simon said. "Except you not being there. Give me the update."

I told him about my move from the emergency shelter to the transitional house. I explained that I could stay until I was done high school. Then they'd help me find an apartment.

Simon asked, "Where is it?"

"Actually I can't tell you —"

"Or you'd have to kill me?" Simon joked.

"Sort of. It's one of the main rules of the house. It's a protected safe space. So I can't give out any information to anyone."

"And that's why we're meeting here," Jeffrey added.

"Yup. Plus I like this place. On weekends, I get kind of bored. So I come out here and watch the people and boats if the weather's good."

"Still glad you didn't take the ferry?" Simon asked.

I nodded. "This place is really good. I mean, it's not a hotel or anything. But I have a great mentor named Adrian. He's funny and really gets me."

"Do you get the school year off?"

"No. I'm at a school close to the house."

"How's that?"

"Okay. I'd rather be with you guys. But there's something nice about not being known. A clean slate."

"Sounds like a sweet deal," Jeffrey said.

"Out of all the other options, it is. For me."

I told Simon and Jeffrey that I would never forget how they both helped me up when I was down. Even when I thought Simon was betraying me to the principal, deep down I knew he was doing it because he cared. He didn't want to see his best friend on the run.

I reached for a piece of paper in my back pocket. "Oh, I almost forgot to tell you." I held out the paper. "I filed for early emancipation. My mentor supported me and apparently my dad had no issues signing it."

"So you're free?" Simon asked.

"I'm free."

Jeffrey said, "We need to celebrate this."

"Yes!" I pointed a little way down the boardwalk. "That's one of the best hot dog carts in the city."

"Let's do it!" Simon exclaimed.

I led the boys down to the end of the boardwalk. As we got in line, I took in a deep breath and slowly let it out. It felt great to be reunited with my friends. I was glad they knew I had a place to stay. I didn't have to worry anymore about failing to meet my dad's high standards. About being scared and emotionally beat down.

It's not what I hoped or even imagined for myself. I may not be going to the same school as my friends. I may not be living in a house with my parents. But I've learned that I am the only one who can decide who I am and where I live. A house is sometimes just an address. It isn't always a home.

Acknowledgements

Thank you to my family for all your support. Thank you to Carrie, Ashley and the entire Lorimer team. To my editor, Kat, I'm very grateful for your guidance and expertise in all phases of this manuscript.

A very special thank you to the people at the YMCA of Greater Toronto. Thank you for taking the time to meet with me and answering all my questions. The information I received was invaluable and added to the depth of this book.

The YMCA has been providing housing and shelter for at-risk youth for decades. Whether it is family problems, trouble with the law, or just being locked out of the house, they help people stay warm and safe.